The Gentler Gamester

By the Author:

The Education of Chauncey Doolittle

Memory's Keep

Walking Toward Home

Child to the Waters

Poems from Scorched Earth

Our Fathers' Fields

The Classical Origins of Southern Literature

A Carolina Dutch Fork Calendar

Tiller: A Novel

William Faulkner and the Continuity of Southern Letters

The Gentler Gamester

In the Deep Heart's Core: Poems of Tribute and Remembrance (forthcoming)

Edited by the Author

Fireside Tales. Stories of the Old Dutch Fork

Poetry and the Practical, by William Gilmore Simms

The Selected Poems of William Gilmore Simms

Selected Reviews on Literature and Civilization

American Novelists Since World War II

THE GENTLER GAMESTER

James Everett Kibler, Jr.

The Gentler Gamester

Copyright© 2024 by James Everett Kibler, Jr.

ALL RIGHTS RESERVED. No part of this publication may be reproduced, distributed, or transmitted in any form or by any means, including photocopying, recording, or other electronic or mechanical methods, or by any information storage and retrieval system without the prior written permission of the publisher, except in the case of very brief quotations embodied in critical reviews and certain other non-commercial uses permitted by copyright law.

This book is a work of fiction. Names, characters, businesses, organizations, places, events and incidents either are the product of the author's imagination or are used fictitiously. Any resemblance to actual persons, living or dead, events, or locales is entirely coincidental.

Produced in the Republic of South Carolina by

Green Altar Books, an imprint of Shotwell Publishing LLC

Post Office Box 2592

Columbia, South Carolina 29202

www.ShotwellPublishing.com

Cover Design: Boo Jackson

ISBN: 978-1-963506-16-7

FIRST EDITION

10 9 8 7 6 5 4 3 2 1

Contents

01. Rodger and Loutrell 1

02. Never You Just Mind What!
     The Further Adventures of Rodger and Loutrell 5

03. Charlie-T's Almost Trip to Florida 11

04. A Turn of The Wheel 15

05. That Goddess Blind 21

06. Nadeen 27

07. Loutrell Turns Epistolary 33

08. Dads and Lads 37

09. Search 45

10. Miss Eustacia 49

11. The Sudden Scholar 53

12. A Chance Meeting 57

13. The Realms of Gold 63

14. Portable Property 69

15. Loutrell and The Jalapeño 73

16. Swift Transitions 77

17. Taking Stock 83

18. Doge 87

19. Opening Doors 95

20. Celebration 103

Epilogue 113

About the Author 117

Be he ne'er so vile,
This day shall gentle his condition.
—Henry V

One

Rodger and Loutrell

Rodger And Loutrell were best friends, but they didn't always communicate too well. This was the case in spite of all the talking Loutrell did, or maybe because of it. Loutrell came from a family of talkers. Getting a word in at family gatherings was not easy. It was said that if you lost your breath, you lost your place. It had gotten so extreme with Loutrell, that he was now one of those sorts who really didn't need a conversation. He could talk to any quiet object that stayed still long enough. It was better if the object could listen, but in a pinch any object would do, moving or otherwise. He sort of talked inside his head, kind of addressing himself and not even looking outside at anyone or anything, but you could hear him rattling on. People always joked and said you couldn't get inside his brain because it was so small, there wasn't room enough in it for himself.

This talkativeness was not the case with Rodger and his family. They hardly said a word at all. Charlie-T, Rodger's young cousin, whom the two tried to help out when the poor fellow needed it (and he always usually did) was just as silent as Rodger. The adjective "taciturn" wouldn't quite cover the situation with either of them.

Loutrell's wife had left him when the nest got empty (no wonder). The children were gone off to jobs in Columbia. About his only social life was church on Sunday. He envied Reverend Walker the more than an hour he had to talk uninterrupted save the occasional amen.

Because Loutrell was alone now, when he did meet someone, he was driven to talk even more than he would have ordinarily. Get him on a little caffeine, and he was like a runaway train. No need to try and stop him. Rodger was the perfect companion because he didn't say absolutely anything. Rodger was like that around everybody, even Charlie-T, but doubly so around Loutrell. He was very patient too and could sit for hours watching the proverbial paint peel. Rodger and Loutrell. It was a match made in heaven.

Loutrell had a beat-up old Glassmaster and a homemade boat trailer he and Rodger had welded together from a thrown-away hundred-year-old truck body. They'd done a right competent job considering the throw-away parts they'd used. This fine summer day, Loutrell had picked Rodger up to go bass and crappie fishing on Lake Moultrie. He'd tied his and Rodger's cane poles neatly under the boat seats. Loutrell as usual talked all the way and Rodger listened, his eyes half shut in that customary squint of his, and answering only in grunts and monosyllables to show he was at least still half awake. He was practicing that fine gift of his to go trance-like, eyes glazed, and with absolutely nothing on his mind and not a care in the world.

The lake was as smooth as glass and a grey haze made the distant moss-draped cypress and tupelo look like dark watercolour blurs blending into mist. Loutrell had packed two snap-top tins of sardines and a sleeve of saltines, so they could spend the whole day.

The fishing was ordinary. They caught several nice crappies and a couple of small rock bass and put them in a spackling bucket to take home. The sound of them occasionally splashing around and the lapping of the water against the boat's sides were about all you could hear—other than Loutrell. Only a few outboards were

The Gentler Gamester

on the lake today. Their corks bobbed without being bothered by another boat's aggravating wake. The worms Loutrell had dug for bait were doing their duty. All in all, it was a picture perfect day.

I met Loutrell in front of the Piggly Wiggly about 4:30 that afternoon. We called it the Social Pig. It was where everybody gathered in town. He was just back the fourteen miles from the lake with the boat trailer behind him. He'd just pulled up to the Pig parking lot and hailed me with his usual loud greeting and cascade of talk.

"Afternoon. You fine? Me too, but a little tired. Looks like you finally washed that truck. Mr. John's finally got mine fixed. Took him enough time and after three tries to get it right. But finally. His wife's in the hospital with gall stones and a kidney infection. Says he needs more work to pay bills. You got you a good mechanic? Bet you have. You ever need engine work and you don't have to have it done right away, then Mr. John's your man. What you been doing? How come I aint seen you in awhile? Me and Rodger been fishing. Sunny all day. Good fishing weather. Not a whole pack of folks on the lake. Caught us a nice mess of fish. You ever get to fish anymore? I know you use to like to. But life goes on whether you want it to or not. Would you believe, Rodger drowsed off and likened to fall out of the boat one time. Don't know what I'm gonna do with him. You ever done that? Bet you have. Almost lost our fish. Nearly turned the boat over. Just dozed off to sleep sitting there. He sure did, though he claims on a stack of bibles that he aint done it. Told him he better swear on a stack of telephone books or he was sure gonna go to hell. Should have seen him today! He gets so excited when he catches a fish that you'd swear it was his first time. Well, you know Rodger. Don't need to say no more. Had us a good ol' time."

This went on a full five minutes with me not answering except to nod and be pleasant. Loutrell said he'd wanted to stay longer on the lake but Rodger had a few chores to do before dark, so they'd come on home. And that's why they were pulling in so early this afternoon. He was taking Rodger to his pickup there in the parking lot. He said Rodger needed a good talking to on the way home because he'd heard Rodger had been doing some things last week he hadn't ought to be. Never you mind what. Loutrell said he'd given Rodger pure down home.

Finally, I just had to override Loutrell with a question. It took some doing. "But where's Rodger?" I asked.

Loutrell craned his neck and checked the truck's muddy side mirror, then jerked half way around and looked through the truck's mud-splattered back window to find no Rodger, and no boat either. Seems he'd forgotten to fasten the boat down when they'd got it on the trailer and it had stayed in the lake when the trailer pulled out from under it.

Rodger had been helping from inside the boat and just stayed there because he always liked to ride back home in the boat on a pretty day. No doubt he preferred the relative peace and quiet and could doze and daydream at ease, despite the fact that Loutrell would now and then talk loud to him anyway from inside the cab, head craning around so as to endanger both their lives. And Loutrell was surprised Rodger wasn't there because, as he said, he'd talked to him all the way home.

When Loutrell retraced his route, he found Rodger still in the boat at the lake's edge where he'd pulled off and left him over an hour ago. Rodger hadn't moved and was looking straight ahead, eyes half open in that squint of his. In fact, with the warm sun on his back, he'd taken the opportunity to have another late afternoon snooze. He didn't relish the farm chores he had to do when he got home anyway.

When he got the chance, Rodger expressed himself not in the least concerned that Loutrell had left him. As he said, he didn't worry. He reckoned that when Loutrell missed his boat, he'd miss him too and at least come back after his boat. Loutrell wouldn't leave that boat to chance, no sirree, me in it to protect it or not. No big deal. Besides, he still had half a sleeve of saltines and he and the fish in the bucket had been keeping themselves company. They were all just taking advantage of a little quiet time.

Two

Never You Just Mind What!
The Further Adventures of Rodger and Loutrell

Rodger had gotten in real trouble this time with Mr. Chance Stately. Mr. Chance owned the Big House of the neighborhood complete with startling white columns, lush dark camellias, and magnolia trees you could smell a mile away in May and June. It wasn't for the smell of magnolias, however, that Rodger and his cousin Charlie-T lingered around. To keep Rodger's Charlie-T Gilyard from being confused with Charlie-T Seabrook, they all called Rodger's cousin Charlie-T from Elloree. It had a kind of poetic ring, a kind of ironic Byronic appellation in keeping with Charlie-T's amatory misadventures with members of the female kind.

For truth to tell, Charlie-T was too bashful around women to ever look one in the eye. His tongue would get tangled up, his face would burn red and he'd stumble off, his eyes fixed on the ground. Bashful wasn't an adequate word to describe what he was. There was no wonder he hadn't any friends.

With behavior like that, he was a puzzle folks his age didn't think it was worth figuring out. They just dismissed him as weird old Charlie-T., and that was that. He was as close to invisible as a person could be. He really didn't mind having no friends; he felt it safer that way.

Charlie-T hadn't had much of a showing in his twenty-four years. His father had left his mama when he was three. He still didn't know where his dad was or what had become of him. Sometimes Charlie-T wondered if he was dead or alive. Most often, he pictured him in jail, the image maybe conjured up from something his mama said. She was always angry when the subject of her husband arose. She got so furious that Charlie-T soon learned not to bring him up at all. The only thing that would settle her down was a pack of cigarettes and a couple of beers.

He had a torn little yellowing photo of his dad that he kept in his drawer. He sometimes took it out and looked at him. The favor between them was there, no disputing that—tall, light haired, and slim. His dad wore cut-off camo pants and a camo ball cap turned around. He hadn't shaved in a few days and had a big grin. The world counted him a handsome man. All Charlie-T knew was that his dad had worked for the phone company as a line technician. Folks said he must have fallen in love with long distance and was gone. His mama said good riddance, that if this country could put a man on the moon, wish they'd put them all up there, starting with him. On the subject of men, she was bitter as gall.

When he was seven, his mama just up and left one cold morning with a heavy frost on the ground. She'd packed her few belongings while Charlie slept and cleared out without so much as a word. All he could see were her footsteps that left dark melted prints in the frost. They led toward town. He followed them till the sun melted them and they were gone..

Oma-Lynn Thomas, his aged grandmother, took him in and did her best to raise him on her severely limited resources until her death when he was fourteen. Rodger was his cousin on his mother's side, and he was all Charlie's only known kin. Rodger tried to see him through high school. Charlie-T didn't rank at the rock bottom of his class, but he was no whiz. No one was surprised that his classmates didn't vote him the one most likely to succeed. In fact, they didn't vote him anything. It was like he wasn't even there, and he didn't mind.

In his senior year, his cousin had helped Charlie get a few odd jobs. One of these was helping harvest and load watermelons for Mr. Chance Stately. The all-day lifting in the Carolina Lowcountry August sun was something only a young fellow or the Mexican migrant farm workers would do. For most around, welfare looked good next to that. Sometimes half dehydrated, Charlie-T hallucinated and pictured watermelons as his only true friends.

Mr. Chance grew the best, sweetest, and most abundant watermelons in the country, a full twenty acres, and he hired Rodger to market the picked melons at an Express Mart filling station parking lot at the Greeleyville exit on Interstate 95. This was the Yankee express route to South Florida and Rodger set up to sell. The travellers had money and didn't haggle over the price as much as the locals did. The locals had a reason though, as Rodger concluded, because he knew they didn't have a whole lot to haggle with. From the looks of the cars these travellers drove, they didn't have to worry much about the next meal. Their worst fault was a kind of shortness and abruptness of manner that matched their clipped speech like semi-automatic rifle fire, and came across as unfriendly and stuck-up.

But it got reported back to Mr. Chance that Rodger and the boys that helped him, Charlie-T included, young men whose testosterone flowed a little too freely and had more of it than brains, had been using the melons for immoral purposes—his melons at that! They'd cut out a plug, use, and put the plug back, and the unsuspecting traveller-purchaser was none the wiser until the next day when they'd wake up at breakfast in West Palm Beach, Orlando, or Boca Raton when they learned the ways of some country folk who didn't take kindly to Northerners very much. It seemed that some of these boys who sold plugged watermelons had heard tell how Yankees had behaved right here where they lived during the Late Unpleasantness. They could believe the stories too from the ways of the travellers they met today. As the locals said, like father, like son, the apple don't fall too far from the tree, and the sins of the fathers get visited on the young'uns' watermelons.

So it got back to Mr. Chance, and poor old Rodger got the reputation of being the local Midnight Melon Molester, when, in fact, it wasn't him but his weird young cousin Charlie-T. Guilt by both kin and association, he reckoned. It was Rodger who'd recommended him for the job.

And Charlie-T and Mr. Chance had already locked horns when Mr. Chance declared that next year he was going to try planting the new yellow-meat kind. Charlie-T disapproved and confided to Rodger that yellow watermelons was unnatural and he didn't date no furriners. Loutrell said that Rodger should have suspected right then that something was going on.

Well, it all came to a crisis when Mr. Chance had the field watched one bright night of a full Carolina moon, and caught Charlie-T red-handed, or exhibiting his own moon, to be more precise. The sheriff's deputy, who tried hard to keep a straight face, took poor Charlie-T in to the Williamsburg County Jail. Mr. Chance insisted on pressing charges, but naming the charge was more difficult than they'd thought. It wasn't exactly theft because Charlie-T didn't take nothing. As he said, whatever he was, he warn't no thief. In that department, his grandma and Sunday school had done well.

Enter Rodger and Loutrell. They found Charlie-T a silver-tongued lawyer in Columbia with a long foreign name, and who talked about as much as Loutrell without saying half as much. He was sharp in the ways of the law, however, and got Charlie-T off scot-free on a technicality. The charge Mr. Chance and the sheriff finally settled on was beastiality, but the court ruled that Charlie-T should go free because a melon ain't no beast. There was good logic in that, uncommon as that commodity was in the decisions of the usual court case. Seems Charlie-T's lawyer had found a precedent from a case of melon molesting in McCarthy, Tennessee, near Knoxville, some years ago. As we said before, he was a sharp one and well-read in all sorts of books..

The little lesson seemed to have taught Charlie-T sufficiently well, so all were happy, Mr. Chance included, and that ended Charlie-T's midnight watermelon molesting episodes, at least for a while. But even though he vowed he'd sworn off Mr. Chance Stately's melons, Loutrell had heard of late that Charlie-T was seen hanging around Mr. Seymour Bright's cantaloupe patch. "Oh, Lord, what next!" Loutrell was overheard to exclaim.

Even though the rumours died down and Charlie-T kept a low profile, he'd single-handedly created a lasting legacy in Williamsburg County. The old joke still goes around about Ag college boys at Clemson: "Clemson, where men are men, and sheep are scared" now adapted to Charlie-T and the local heath: "Williamsburg County, where melons are terrified." Old Mr. Deeter, the ninety-three year-old sage of the community, had a piece of advice for the boys around there about stock-diddling and the likes. "Boys," he said, "just find you a long-leaf pine knot-hole. It don't tell no tales." But Charlie-T, bless his heart, had sense enough to counter that he reckoned that watermelons didn't neither.

You can imagine that the local practical jokers couldn't resist having a little fun at Charlie-T's and Rodger's expense. One morning Rodger got up to find a pair of watermelons on his front steps with a note attached, "For you and Charlie-T. Your own personal melons," using the ad for the personal pan pizza at the local pizza chain. There were even songs—ditties called "Charlie Went a-Courtin' in the Melon Patch," "Watermelon Man," and "Charlie, Don't Take Your Watermelon to Town."

All this ran its course into juvenile banality, but Rodger still bore the stigma of association with midnight melon romancing and was not like to live it down for a long time. Loutrell found it best to nip any talk of the subject in the bud with a quick "never you mind what," and this was a difficult thing for him, as you might gather, knowing how dearly much he had always loved to talk. This time for him for once, silence was golden.

As for poor old Charlie-T—Rodger and Loutrell distanced themselves from the true source of the problem and didn't encourage him hanging around. Charlie-T still got himself a good many odd jobs, the kinds that nobody else would take, but they never again involved a watermelon field. You could often see him at the Feed and Seed lifting heavy burlap bags, his ball cap turned round.

He wasn't lazy. You had to give him that. He was strong too, a pretty good specimen of a man like his handsome daddy. His daddy and mama had at least given him good genes. Precious little else maybe, but his strength got him a lot of heavy lifting jobs where machines couldn't go or were too valuable to risk.

Three

Charlie-T's Almost Trip to Florida

All Rodger had to do was look at his cousin. He confided to Loutrell that the seat of Charlie-T's pants looked like a family of darkies had just moved out. He was as lean as a hound in the doldrums of the dog days. For some young bucks, that meant they might be chasing does and not getting any sleep; but as Loutrell said, just the opposite had to be true of Charlie-T. He still couldn't get a woman to give him a second look.

The problem was this: it was deep into September and the annual Watermelon Festival in Hampton County was already become a fading memory, the watermelon harvests all across the Lowcountry had been accomplished, and a great scarcity of the fruit had made a veritable desert of the land—at least to Charlie-T.

Had Rodger and Loutrell, bless their hearts, known the verse of that felicitously named English poet, Sir John Suckling, they'd had the ideal phrase, "Why so pale and wan, fond lover?" That certainly seemed to describe Charlie-T to a T.

He sat a lot alone outside the Express Mart off Interstate 95, where he'd had one of Mr. Chance's watermelon stands back in the halcyon days of last summer, remembering those days, and casting longing looks southward down the asphalt lanes. He was even heard to sigh a deep love-sick sounding sigh as an eighteen-wheeler with Florida tags sped unheedingly down the road into the grey-blue. He sometimes got to humming the lyrics of a popular country song that played incessantly inside: *Every storm runs out of rain.* He'd seen a lot of thunderstorms and knew it was true. He wondered if that would ever happen to him.

From one of the migrant farm workers in their seasonal travelling southward, he heard tales of the more than usual abundant second crop of watermelons this year in the Sunshine State. He knew the late harvest was just peaking there now as he sat sighing and pining away.

The world was passing him by, he mumbled to himself over the noise of traffic. He didn't usually drink or have extra money for beer, but he'd had a job moving some refrigerators this morning and had a little to spend. With the courage plucked, or more accurately, gulped from a couple of cold Ice Houses, in the tall cans, just as he liked them, he decided to take the situation firmly in hand.

He hitched a ride with a salesman out of McBee, who was headed down I-95 to Orlando. This good Samaritan could instantly tell a fellow traveller in need. Though the driver was friendly enough and tried to get him to talk, Charlie-T didn't have much to say. He told Charlie the latest news from his hometown, pronouncing it *Mack.be,* with the stress on the first syllable, like they did back home as he said.

Charlie-T didn't have to go all the way to Florida, however, for about a short four hours into his journey, his eyes opened upon the Elysian stretches of flat sandy watermelon fields green and grey striped with fruit far as the eye could see. This was in southernmost Georgia a few miles shy of the Florida line.

"Just lemme out here," he told the puzzled Samaritan. There wasn't a filling station, McDonald's, or house in sight. But Samaritan obliged.

Well, it wasn't long before the country got enough of Charlie-T. Ludowici, Alma, and Baxley, Georgia, had no use for the likes of him. Seems they had their own local home-grown melon molesters like Charlie-T' and didn't need no more. Truth to say, in fact, one was way too much. As for Charlie-T's Bacon County counterparts, they said they didn't need no competition, and especially from anybody the likes of Charlie-T. Charlie-T considered them downright unfriendly, and in particular them four rough Crews family boys.

Hitchhiked back home, Charlie-T looked the worse for wear. Loutrell and Rodger hardly knew him when they found him sitting bareheaded on the bench one foggy morning outside the Feed and Seed. In fact they were startled. It was as if a ghost had suddenly materialised out of the November mist. He had a split lip, a swollen eye, and several dark bruises on his forearm and face. He walked real stiff and had a hard time sitting down.

Loutrell hailed him saying that weeks back when the manager of the Express Mart had told them he'd been last seen headed for Florida, they'd thought he'd done sure enough become one of them snow birds. Charlie-T only shook his head and vowed he'd never leave Williamsburg County ever again, "for love nor money." He had a sort of far-off, embarrassed, tragic sort of look in his eye as if he'd seen too much of the world. "World-weary" didn't quite capture the expression. It went beyond chastened and was more like disappointment tinged with outrage. Whatever the look, Charlie-T was never again quite the same. No better, no worse, just changed.

He'd never say what happened down there in that strange land, but he vowed to himself, watermelons or not, that he'd sure enough never go back. He wasn't known widely as a man of mystery, but in this instance, so he became. Loutrell joked to Rodger that he reckoned the experience, whatever it was, had done cured him from wanting to turn snow bird. They'd of late got to noticing that anytime anyone mentioned the word Florida, he would wince.

Of those weeks in September into October, Charlie-T always referred to them as his Almost Trip to Florida, but would never give details, and Rodger refused to press the issue, fearing he would. "Sometimes best not to know," he told Loutrell. Charlie-T's scrapes and bruises healed. Whatever the ruckus, he'd fought game. Charlie was once overheard to say that there were four of them. The subject seldom came up, but if it happened to, Loutrell would only shake his head and say that he figured that whatever befell Charlie-T down there in Almost Florida, was only the watermelon's rightful revenge.

Four

A Turn of The Wheel

After his return from down south, Charlie-T made himself scarce for quite a while. Seems he liked the sound of being called mystery man. He was seen around town here and there, ball cap turned around like his dad's in the little photo, but he didn't often visit his usual haunts. He was hardly ever seen seated outside the Express Mart anymore. He didn't stay put anywhere even if you could spot him and try to pin him down.

At first, Rodger and Loutrell thought he might have some sort of job picking up or delivering something or other. He'd bought himself a used Silverado, dented and scraped a bit, but it was nice enough—a lot newer and better than Loutrell's. They wondered where the money came from. At first they thought it was from the mystery job, but Charlie-T was never seen to haul or pick up anything. They noted that he didn't wear no special uniform. Pizza delivery boys had to wear that little hat and he had none, just the same old ball cap turned around, like always. It was a new one though, with GAMECOCKS. BACK TO BACK NATIONAL BASEBALL CHAMPS on the crown.

Charlie-T had got himself a lanky, short-haired black and white spotted dog, that he called Shugg—short for Sugar, Rodger reckoned. That's all he hauled in that new Silverado. Shugg was always on the front seat by Charlie-T, sitting on her hind haunches looking regally from front windshield to side window—altogether dignified. First time Rodger saw her he could have counted her ribs; now she was obviously sleek, well-groomed, pampered, and well-fed. At the Express Mart, Charlie-T bought some peanuts to put in his co-cola and paid for them with a twenty. He use to have to count out his change.

Mr. Lou-Dabbs Porcher, the owner of the Feed and Seed, told Rodger that yesterday his nephew had turned down a heavy lifting unloading job. Mr. Lou-Dabbs said that Charlie-T was polite about it and thanked him, but wouldn't be persuaded even by time and half salary, then a double-time raise. Mr. Lou-Dabbs asked Charlie T, "What gives?" A shrug of the shoulders and a respectful little sideways nod of the head was Charlie T's reply. Instead of looking down at his feet, this time Charlie T looked him straight in the eye. Mr. Lou-Dabbs couldn't recollect that Charlie T's eyes were blue. He reckoned he'd never really seen them before. They were electric blue and such that you remembered them.

Yes, Mr. Lou-Dabbs, Rodger, and Loutrell had found Charlie-T changed, as they said, but then they hadn't seen the half of it yet. With a little more knowledge, they could declare he was *shore 'nough* changed, but even after that, they still hadn't fathomed the extent. They could see clearly that the change seemed to be reflected in his face and bearing. He was overheard to tell Mr. Lou-Dabbs one day that when you throw a rock into Lake Moultrie, it ain't happy 'til it sinks to the bottom. He figured he'd touched that low place down on the Florida-Georgia line.

Truth to tell, folks were finally realizing he wasn't an ugly or goofy looking fellow anyway. It was just the clumsy and curious way he acted that made him appear dumb. It was hard to see through that. And he always used to be looking down at his feet. He'd never meet your gaze. If he ever had to look up, he'd wince and look away as if he wasn't good enough to look at you in the face. A psychologist would just have deemed him shy but I expect it was more than that too. He held himself a little bent over and kind of stoop shouldered. He looked as if he was trying to make himself smaller, scrunching himself up, maybe not to be seen. Of late, Rodger noticed, he was standing upright, shoulders back. He'd not realized how tall his cousin was, a full six foot two. He walked different too and with a deliberate gate. It was like he had somewhere to go, maybe even an important place to be.

He'd started dressing better. Leather replaced worn out gym shoes that had shown his toes poking through holes in his socks. If clothes made the man, some kind of creation was going on. Loutrell and Rodger could only shake their heads and wonder, wide-eyed. He still kept paying for little things with twenty dollar bills and a c-note a time or two.

Loutrell ascribed Charlie-T's transformation to his Almost Trip to Florida. Rodger didn't know, but wondered if Reverend Hawkins had had anything to do with it, but the good Reverend said not that he knew. Under Miss Oma-Lynn's care, he had already been baptized in the black water river behind the church a good ten years ago. He was now coming to Sunday morning service again—sporadically at first, then more regularly.

Nothing could have amazed anyone more than when Charlie-T drove up to the Feed and Seed sharing the front seat of a brand new, newly polished Silverado this time, and with Shugg and Nadeen.

Nadeen was a petite, quiet, flaxen-haired beauty with peach-blossom skin. Pretty as the spring flowers on her cotton dress. From the looks of her, she'd have been considered a catch for anyone around there, and especially for someone like Charlie-T, reputation for melon-molesting or not. Next time he drove to the Piggly Wiggly for groceries, Nadeen accompanied him inside. The time after that, the check-out girl noticed Nadeen had on a wedding ring with one of the nicest rocks she'd ever seen. *Cubic zirconia* the cashier said to herself, but little did she know; it was real. Two and a half carats at the least and maybe three. It was an eye-catching ring.

Folks really did begin to wonder when the couple moved out of Miss Oma-Lynn's trailer to a very nice house on one of Kingstree's quietest, moss-covered live-oak shaded streets. They knew no one had died and left him anything. His grandma had sure never owned anything but decency and pride and Charlie-T had squandered that. And even though that went a long way in Kingstree, it didn't pay no bills. Folks at Oma-Lyn's church knew she and Charlie-T sometimes went without, but they hardly knew the extent.

So now with Charlie-T's sudden largesse, the unkind among them jumped straight to the conclusion that he'd have to be dealing drugs or manufacturing them. He must have got some Florida connection. They wondered where the meth lab was. The sheriff took note and kept his eyes open. Charlie-T heard the rumors, but declared to himself that even at his lowest, he'd never sunk that low.

And folks in the community marveled that he still didn't seem to have a job, unless he worked at night or at home. And it got around that several times he was seen to break a hundred dollar bill at the gasoline pump.

Although some stiff necks turned, Nadeen started attending church with Charlie-T and demonstrated quite a beautiful soprano in the hymns. Her English was becoming almost as standard as Charlie-T's. She was as quick to pick up anything new that they'd ever seen.

Folks wondered and wondered and Charlie-T thought this was good. A community always needed something to talk about—a puzzle—a riddle in a bottle to try to figure out. Well, Charlie-T was this game for quite some time, and he was glad to oblige. Most of the townsfolk wished him the best whatever the cause. A few of the Feed and Seed regulars, when they spotted him around town, said that he'd even been seen to smile, and in their memory, that was a first time. One of the ladies noted that he had nice regular teeth, and not from the dentist, that's for sure, she added.

The picture puzzle came together gradually, a little here, a little there, a bit at a time. First off they learned from Charlie-T's cousin that Nadeen was a mail-order bride. She'd come from Eastern Europe where she'd had a hell of a time in a land at war. The cousin knew because he'd helped Charlie-T get the papers together and done everything lawyer-legal in the federal courthouse in Columbia. All they knew from the cousin was that it had cost quite a bundle, and this peaked curiosities all the more. The cousin had done his duty right. "It's amazing what money can do," he declared, "And how fast." Nadeen was legal and soon to be naturalized. This laid all the gossip to rest that Charlie-T must have married money, the first thing they thought when they saw Nadeen and the ring.

Charlie T dropped the *T* and *ie* off his name and came to be Charles Gilyard. Nadenia Durakovic became a simple Nadeen. She soon had her driving license and could drive Charlie's truck. Her husband got her a new SUV, ready for their first child. The Piggly Wiggly cashier soon noted that it wouldn't be long. She now paid for the groceries with a gold Visa Card, and it was never denied.

At this point, Rodger and Loutrell went about in amaze with their mouths open wide half the time. Looks like Charlie-T—. Urrrr, Mr. Charles Thomas Gilyard, excuse me!—had distanced them, had left them far behind. For all practical purposes, he was out of their lives. But the puzzle remained.

Five

That Goddess Blind

*Her foot is on a spherical stone,
which rolls and rolls.*

The answer to the riddle was simple enough. It sounds unlikely, but some things like this do happen; they just do. The fickle, giddy one who stands upon the restless, rolling wheel had looked Charlie-T's way, and though he was invisible to everybody around him, he wasn't to her.

The day that he left for Florida, he was in a real confused state of mind. He'd figured he'd wasted time and now time was wasting him. He knew one line from Shakespeare's *Richard* play, and those words about time wasting a man was it. Echoes from Miss Carlisle's senior English class sometimes came out of nowhere when he'd least expected them. He had liked Miss Carlisle. Although he'd always sat scrunched down on the very last row and never said a word, she had always seemed to regard him as real. As for her assignments, he always did them, when he blew those in other courses off.

He tried to convince himself that day at the Express Mart that it was melons in Florida he wished for, but knew that if he was honest with himself, it was more. He just wasn't clear what he craved.

Then there it was at the Express Mart—the bouncing red ball sign! Powerball. He'd never played the state lottery a single time before, but today the world was teetering wildly, his mind whirring and whirling, and he in a kind of daze. Without thinking, he plopped down the two dollars. In his worn out wallet, there weren't but three more behind. One ticket was all. Again without thinking, he added the extra dollar to increase the payload. That left two dollars between him and an empty pinched belly. His dazed state of mind had even blocked that out and he walked in a daze. Maybe it was hunger that made him weak, but it went even beyond that.

It wasn't only his world spinning, but fortune's own unpredictable wheel. It creaked on its ancient supports as it lurched to turn with a harsh grating sound.

The man from McBee came in; Charlie-T got his ride.

His month's stay over, he was back home. A few days after his return, he sat uneasily on his old bench outside the Express Mart. He still shifted his weight from side to side and recalled the injuries he'd received. Thinking over his misadventures on the Florida-Georgia line, he knew one thing for certain sure now from experience, that life does that to you sometimes, and when your pants are down.

The buzz had died down here, and things gotten back to normal, but a month ago, it seemed the Express Mart was for a brief moment the centre of the globe. At the same time he was at his lowest in Bacon County, Georgia, television trucks and newspaper men waited their turn here in line. They swarmed the scene. Recorders recorded, cameras aimed and panned, and flashes popped. Everybody waited expectant, breaths held, as if for the appearance of a new sovereign lord. The Powerball winner who'd bought the winning ticket here at the Express Mart had chalked up a cool 789 million, but had not come forth to claim his prize.

In the grimy back pocket of his worn-out jeans, witness to so many misadventures, and in that tattered old wallet, sweat-soaked then dried, nestled the talisman ticket, bearing all the numbers and even the magical red Powerball herself—waiting her own time to come forth and be in the sun, like the tendrilled hooded green sheath of a patient and silent watermelon seed secreted in the ground.

How easy to have lost it, wallet and all, had it stolen, or tossed it away. Yet it was tucked away safely, luckily forgotten, to sleep there unseen until resurrection after a purgatorial span. It was one chance in many billions, they said, and the stuff of a story so unreal not even a fiction writer would touch it, and certainly no reader would abide such a *deus ex machina* in the most outlandish plot.

Poor old Charlie-T. His breath was taken from him as he read the numbers at least a good six times. Then out with the gentle folded hills of the landscape spinning and dissolving before him, he went to tell only the skies. In truth, he had no one to tell.

When he found a starving Shugg cast off by the side of the road near his trailer, he told the dog and only the dog. Shugg was the first to know. She barely had strength to lick his hand. He took her in and thawed her a cubed deer steak that Rodger had given him back in hunting season time and which he was saving for a special meal. If this wasn't special, he'd like to know what was. A millionaire and a new dog in the same afternoon! He told Shugg that like Grandma Oma-Lynn used to say, "Every dog has its day" and he reckoned that this day, there were two who most certainly would have theirs. Shugg in gulping her food still took time between swallows to look at the face of her benefactor. How could Charlie-T forget that! From that moment they became friends.

Then Charlie-T ran him a tub full of hot water and had him a good soak. He submerged his whole body, and even slowly dunked his head under several times. He shaved off his copper colored growth of beard, then after adding more hot water, dozed in the tub.

When he woke up, the water had cooled, so he walked out back with a towel around him and burned his clothes. He dried outside in the late autumn sun, then burned the towel. He watched the fire as the flames crept along the fibers and blackened them to ash. A swirling column of smoke rose to the sky. He was not bothered by his nakedness as the awareness came over him that he stood before his Maker as he had been born, a new man with the world before him.

When he came in, there lay Shugg on his chair on his threadbare flannel shirt. Shugg raised her head and looked at him with heavy intent eyes as if to ask if this was okay.

Much as he'd have liked to, he'd never had a dog before. Miss Oma-Lyn said that with their limited resources they couldn't afford human food, much less dog food, not to mention a vet. "You going to have a dog," she told him, "You got to take responsibility."

Still, Charlie-T knew dog nature well, from other people's dogs, and Rodger and Loutrell had often said that they thought he could read a dog's mind.

"That shirt's yours. I won't be needing it no more," he said in a tone of voice which Shugg understood.

So there was Shugg—one minute, thrown away, starving, shaking with fear, on the outside with the fickle sky as her only ceiling, and the next minute, inside, clean, dry, warm, and steak-fed, on her new master's favorite flannel shirt and in his chair.

Charlie-T made it to Columbia the next day with a man at the Feed and Seed from whom he bummed a ride. He didn't say why he needed the ride.

At the lottery office the ticket was verified. After profuse congratulations, the head administrator drove him to the bank and got him some cash, fronted him fifteen thousand in twenty and hundred dollar bills so he'd be able to pay for a taxi ride home, and, as the lottery official said, for some spending money to tide him over until the necessary paper-work could be done. This would take some time. Charlie-T had to make certain decisions, and then he'd receive the bulk of his prize. He decided to take the whole prize, and not the installments. Life was too unexpected short sometimes and he didn't have faith that government would last much longer either with all the tomfoolery it was up to.

He chose not to be named as the winner. He was liking this role of mystery man. And it was nobody's business but his and Shugg's.

Again the world seemed to lurch on its axis and the landscape whirl as his San Jose taxi cab sped down the congestion of an eight lane Elmwood Avenue out to Interstate 26, leaving the burnishing copper dome of the State House behind.

He saw for the very first time the shining glossy leaves of the magnolias along the highway leading in and out of the city. Strange, though he'd been on this route several times, the trees had never cheered him before. He supposed he'd never really seen them. It was as if they'd never been there at all and now somehow they had suddenly materialised. Such was the luxury of the wheel's happy turn. He'd not realized it then, but it was a truth he would live to know.

Every once in a while, the voice of old Miss Carlisle would come to him with a line or a scrap or a phrase. She had made much of Shakespeare's day and its understanding of Dame Fortune's wheel, and when she did, she always seemed to look at him, seeking him out scrunched down in that last row, looking at him like maybe there was the potential of some sort of promise in the words. His Bible teachings were with him too, with the high made low and the low made high, and the reversal of first and last. Charlie-T knew his Beatitudes. Sometimes they had been his only comfort in the hardest times.

Twice lucky for Mr. Charles Thomas Gilyard. He may have had his weird and freakish moments in his short lifetime, but he was never a must-control-everything-freak or a know-it-all. One thing he did know and had always known even in his darkest mood, that life is a miracle; it can't be plotted, charted, predicted, or drawn in a straight line. You lived by faith and at the mercy of your Maker.

God bless you, Charlie-T Gilyard. May you and yours thrive.

Six

Nadeen

Nadeenia Arvos Durakovic came from one of those new countries with unpronounceable names. Without leaving their beds, the citizens had waked up one morning in a new country and to new lives overnight with the sudden and unpredicted Soviet's fall. It was if their world had been determined by an unseen roll of cosmic dice.

In their new minting out of old metals, these countries still had a lot of sorting out to do and there was some rough jostling around. In some countries the transition was easy, but in Nadeen's, war had decimated her small hometown, and her neighbourhood in particular. Her two older brothers had been killed in the fray. Her father had been captured and taken somewhere, place unknown. He may have been killed. Their modest house was missing a wall, the victim of shells.

For a time, what was left of the family lived under the roof and within the three walls, but when the snows of winter came, they moved in with the mother's sister-in-law. She had five little ones of her own under the age of twelve. Food was scarce in the house, and the struggle for survival became increasingly hard. The sister-in-law's husband had also been taken away. Rumor was he had been lined up and shot in the head.

Nadeen was another mouth to feed. She went with her closest friend, a young woman of nineteen, to the nearest large city that for a time was at relative peace. They were recruited by a man who came to their town looking for workers among folks who didn't have much choice but to go. His name was Leopold. Her mother worried, but Leopold had good references from a cousin whom they trusted, so Nadeen and her friend packed their few belongings in canvas bags and were gone. After the door closed, her mother cried and could not be consoled. It was good Nadeenia couldn't see. Going would have been even harder that way.

The two worked in a sewing room. The hours were long and most of their pay went for room and board. Still, there was enough to send to their families back home. Nadeen may not have known it, but it was that which made the difference of her mother and aunt's having enough to stave off hunger and keep the proverbial wolf from the door. And at least they still had a door. Many did not. For their little corner of the world, these were desperate times—a roller-coaster of fortunes from the exhilaration of freedom to violence and want.

After Nadeen and her friend worked at the sewing room for a year, things got better in their home town. Her father got home, roughed up and hungry, but he soon had the remnants of his family with a roof over their heads. To his wife, he looked like he'd aged ten years. He wrote Nadeen she could come home now, but it still could be dangerous and there wasn't much left but ruins in their blackened town. Not even the chance of a job, he feared. News was not good for her aunt. The rumors were correct. Her husband had been killed and she would have to raise the five children alone. Nadeen's father would do all he could.

There had been temptations for Nadeen and her friend in the city, but the two women were smart. Nadeen's common sense told her that when a deal seemed too good to be true, it usually was. Leopold turned out to be honest and fair. They now called him Leo and counted him a friend. He didn't ask anything of them. He'd gotten his lump payment from the employer for bringing the girls in. He warned Nadeen about certain occupations from which to stay clear. She did. The horror stories of girls trapped that way in slavery made her thankful for the little she had.

That little would soon be less. Her girlfriend had gotten engaged to a young man in the city and would soon be moving out and with her went half the rent.

Then she got Charlie's picture from the couple who rented her and her friend their room. It came with a short hand-written letter. Although it was in English, she could figure some of it out. She took it to Leo, who read and spoke English quite well, and he translated it. Leo'd known of such arrangements before, and knew if luck was on their side, they could be good. For Nadeen.

As for herself, she thought it a scam. Wasn't it one of those deals the girls in the sewing room warned her about? No one had that much wealth, at least gotten fair and square. He seemed sincere though, and more than about riches, which she only half believed; but there was something in his words that touched her. She thought he had the loveliest clear blue eyes she'd ever seen. They seemed to be searching the world. She reckoned he was, and she was too. On his lips she detected the promise of a smile. It looked to her like he wanted to, but didn't quite know how and maybe was just afraid to. She knew that feeling well. His expression seemed to show the capacity for hope. That hadn't been killed in her either by circumstances as dire as they'd been.

She had been learning that desperation comes in all sizes and shapes, in all situations, and in all men and women in every nook and cranny of the world. The letter ended with "Give me a chance. I'm alone in the world."

Nadeenia's landlord and wife were employed by an agency who scouted for pretty country girls in her desperate situation. For a large fee and air-fare one way, the agency could promise an American customer a willing bride. After a meeting, if the prospective groom proved unhappy, he paid only for a two-way ticket and the girl came back home.

What had Charlie to lose? Money was no object to him. So they met at the Greenville-Spartanburg airport. Nadeenia was on a jet with lots of German speaking passengers whom she could sometimes understand. They worked locally outside Spartanburg for a big concern and were happy with this part of the world. They found the people kind. For Nadeen, she felt that this boded well.

Charlie couldn't believe his eyes. When the man who accompanied her made the introduction, as was his usual wont, Charlie couldn't find words. As soon as he gained composure and got control he said what he'd been pondering now for a week. Through the translator he let her know from the start that this wouldn't be the usual kind of deal. She could stay if she chose to and he'd help her, love interest or not. No blame from him. He would not force himself on her.

He already had her a small house with one key and they would date like any young couple would. The gentleman who translated for them would give Charlie a comprehending look of admiration every now and then. He'd never experienced this kind of decency before or united such a really handsome young pair. It was clear that he was impressed by the proceedings and at the end of the interview told Charlie so. He went so far as to use the word *gallantry*, a term Charlie only partially understood.

While the two men made their final arrangements, Nadeenia stood apart at a distance watching them, seeing their lips move but not understanding a word. She stood silhouetted against great sheets of plate glass windows sheathed in steel, and out of which she could see the jets on the runway taxying this way and that. Men scurried in luggage carts loading and unloading, rushing to and fro. It reflected a world in love with speed, motion and flux.

Charlie looked at her. He was only half hearing the man explaining details. She held a soiled canvas bag in each hand. What must she be thinking? She was completely at a stranger's mercy in a strange land. Her lips seemed to be moving. He had no way of knowing, but she was praying the *Kyrie* in good church Latin. Charlie took it all in, or at least what he felt she was going through. He figured he'd been there before.

Then the nice man was gone. Charlie remembered that they had shaken hands, he in a sort of daze, and recollected little else. He and Nadeenia drove straight to Kingstree, trying to be pleasant but not saying a word. He was afraid to look at her except with side glances when he thought he wasn't observed. Charlie was use to that, but today somehow he wished he could look straight on.. They got there before sundown. The small house seemed to suit her. He had hired a maid who'd fitted out bedroom and bath and gave the house a feminine touch, all those little things that were lost on him.

He'd personally stocked the kitchen with groceries the day before. Yesterday, he'd gone to the florist for the first time in his life. On the kitchen table, in a new crystal vase, he'd put two long stem roses in bud, one red, one white. It was to be her choice, he made her understand, of which one to take. Red she would keep him; white he would go.

Nadeenia broke into tears at the sight of the full refrigerator when she thought of her family and what she'd left at home.

At that, Charlie thought he'd done something wrong, but she soon clarified her crying in a way that made his heart swell. It was merely the soft touch of the flat palm of her hand to his reddening cheek.

He was reluctant to leave, but gave her the key. More than anything in the world, he wanted to stay. "Nadeenia," he said. "Rest" and folded his hands together and put them to the side of his head in the universal gesture of sleep. He knew she must be awfully tired from the ordeal.

"Tomorrow," he said and made her understand he'd see her the next day, and was gone. On his way, he tuned his new Bose acoustic. The country station was playing "Every Storm Runs Out of Rain." It seemed that the song followed him everywhere he went. He couldn't get it out of his head.

Seven

Loutrell Turns Epistolary

To Mister Charlie-T Gilyard, Kingstree, SC

Dear Charlie-T,

I been here in Pooler, Georgia, now 7 weeks helping Great uncle Rupert Spalding recover from the hospital & his attact. They let him go now 3 weeks back. Yesterday we went out to Tybee & caught us some flounder. Flat as pancakes & eyes on one side. Spooky. But good eats.

I really like them big deep sea fishing boats. They can get after it with their big-ass engines. Declared to Rupert that I wouldn't mind much living round here. The fishing is good. He didn't say nothing to that. I almost took it as a sign.

Uncle Rupert met you and Miss Oma-Lynn up there at church one time. I told him your whole recent story, all about Nay-deen & the new baby boy. He said that unlike <u>Yours Truly</u>, sounds like you aint a scrounger and a moocher no more. He's always full of platitudes. Worse than Reverend Hawkins. Says everybody got to pay his way in this world. Says you don't work & you don't eat. It's simple as that. I reckon that was a hint, but I didn't let on like I heard.

Uncle Rupert is a real joker. He laughs & says, new dog, new truck, new house, new wife, new baby, you must have done won the Lottery, ha, ha, ha. Rupert is always a good one for jokes. He says I ought to ask you for a raise or at least your spare pocket change.

I met Miss Georgia Latina last week. Didn't know they had one. She lives just 5 or 6 miles from Uncle Rupert. Met her at his church. She's a catholic but says baptists is ok. Says, flashing them big brown eyes, it's all the same Jesus you know. She's a looker. Whooee! Always liked them dark-eyed women. Rupert says I ought to be ashamed; I'm old enough to be her grandpa—which I am not. Told him, shucks, I might be old, but I aint dead—like you nearly was with your heart attact 7 weeks ago. All the boys at church say they don't need to court Miss Georgia Latina, just like to take a look at her every once in a while. Going home from church Rupert scolded me saying I didn't need to tell her his and my whole life history. He said that one of my 30 minute rambles would even try the patience of Job, which Miss Georgia Latina certainly aint. Says sometimes I talked so much I was like to give him another attact. So I expect in another month or two, I'll come on back home. Fishing season will be through anyways.

Uncle Rupert says his mama use to have a saying about kin who come to visit, that they's like old fish. It didn't make no sense, but from his tone and expression, I got the drift. Asked him if he remembered old maid Aunt Lula who came to us on a visit & stayed a lifetime. That shut him up tight as a drum.

I hear the preacher this Sunday'll be preaching on lust of the flesh. Wonder if that includes Water Melons Charlie-T, hahaha.

Sincerely,

Your ever faithful, ever devoted,

& most esteemed friend,

Loutrell Decimus Heywood.

In the next week's mail came Charlie's reply to Loutrell.

Kingstree SC

Dear Loutrell,

Charles Jr. is a hand full, but we got a woman to live in. She insists on calling herself a nanny, English style.

Rodger has taken up some of my jobs at the Feed and Seed, those he can handle, that is. It takes a strong back, and he caint lift heavy anymore. Haven't seen him much now I'm a dad. Been thinking a lot about my life these days and have come to the reckoning that there's nothing so becomes a man as modesty and humility. I told Nadeenia the modest and humble are the folks we want to be around now and try to be ourselves.

Speaking of my shameful times, Loutrell, I'm not the man I was.

Sincerely, your old friend,

Charles

Eight

Dads and Lads

He sat at the long mahogany table in the dining room with Shugg at his feet. He didn't move so as not to disturb her. She often slept that way, with her head on his feet. On the sideboard in its crystal vase stood a solitary dried rose, still there despite its dessication, and still vibrantly red. From upstairs he could hear little Charlie making baby noises in the bassinette in the nursery he and Nadeen had converted from one of the second story bedrooms. He could hear nanny Hazel's protestations to the tabby to get out of the nursery or risk execution by broom.

From the kitchen he listened to Nadeen jostling her new copper pans as she worked on dinner. They always tried to eat at noon. She didn't squander time and was efficient at the new restaurant-quality stove. She liked cooking. It was a luxury to have anything in the way of groceries that her heart could desire, and in any quantity.

The house had a large walk-in pantry. Nanny Hazel called it the larder, using the English word for such a room. It had gleaming rows of well-stocked shelves. All this was very new to her. She wondered how anyone could fail to be thankful in this bountiful world she'd just entered. She soon mastered Charlie Sr.'s favorite foods—those he'd been use to from Miss Oma-Lynn. He wasn't hard to please. His only demand was grits at a big breakfast to start the day. His grandma had set the pattern in that as well.

At first Nadeen had trouble with grits. She used a native term to describe them that translated more or less, "Yuk." To that, Charlie replied with mock displeasure in his eye, "Now, don't be dogging my grits, Nadeen." She learned how to fix them from a neighbor—salted just right, sometimes with cheese, sometimes with cream. She knew that there could be bacon or sausage. There could be ham, but the one constant of grits had to remain. And they had to be what he called "fork grits," that is, grits you could eat with a fork and not the runny cream of wheat kind. At times in Charlie's young life, breakfast grits had been just about the only physical constant. It was something that Miss Oma-Lynn could always afford and was more than a comfort food. Sometimes at the end of the month there wasn't anything else but.

Nadeen started humming a folk tune she'd learned as a child. She did that a lot. Charlie reckoned it was a way for just a moment to go back home. He couldn't even imagine how hard it would be to be taken like she was from everything she knew. Sometimes in her sweet musical voice, she would sing the words that Charlie couldn't understand. No matter. He interpreted well, from the trace of a drying tear as she sang. At that, he would sometimes brush the tracks away.

This morning he was wearing a crisply starched and ironed shirt with a button down collar. He loved that feel of order and tidiness on his back. It seemed to gentle him and make him sit up straight. He felt what a good thing it was to have a fresh clean shirt every day, some days maybe even two. He got so he really missed it if he didn't have one.

He had gotten to liking French cuffs too. He had the time to fold and clip them and dress properly. Time. What a luxury. What a luxury to slow down. You could pay attention to little things.

The couple now had a cook, by the name of Varzine, who lived in the little guest house on the back green. The cook's house came with the place. Varzine helped Nadeen out in the kitchen when Nadeen wanted her to, but also did their laundry up nicely and kept the house clean. She still hung clothes in the Carolina sun on a clothes-line in the old-time way because she said it made them smell and feel fresh like nothing else could. It was a big house and too much for Nadeen, especially with a new baby, and another on the way.

Hazel could be a shop-a-holic if the couple didn't sometimes rein her in. Often she and Varzine conspired to introduce a new luxury they thought the couple should have. Nadeen sometimes pretended to scold, but Charlie would just smile. He allowed the two a household account, and kept it full. They could themselves write checks without asking him. The women correctly interpreted this as keep on doing what you do until I tell you otherwise.

One of those extras for him was the finest 200's thread-count cotton shirts—the best money could buy—soft and smooth. Hazel loved to shop on King Street in Charleston and one day brought home a couple dozen of these in whites and pastel blues. She found them at Ben Silver's, her favorite men's store down town. Varzine didn't grumble. She liked starching and ironing for him. He always acted like he appreciated so much everything she did. They both loved making a fuss over him, and they wouldn't think of sending the couple's clothes to a laundry. "Breaks all the buttons," Varzine complained. Charlie looked good in the clothes and did justice to them. Neither Hazel nor Varzine had children of their own, and they took pride in Charlie's appearance. With Charlie's new life, they swore he stood up straighter and looked even taller than he had before.

Hazel, despite her family's rebellious Irish background, was an anglophile. Ben Silver's supplied the English country style that she wanted for Charles and Nadeen. The store stocked merchandise from hacking jackets to ascots, enameled gold cuff-links, and crested English regimental ties. Even though Charles didn't smoke, Hazel bought him a fine English smoking jacket, which he sometimes wore for her sake. Every time he put it on, he smiled at the irony. He never really liked the smell of tobacco. His mother was a chain smoker and the house always smelled of nicotine and had a residue of tar on everything. One of his few memories was that her right index finger was always stained. Dear Hazel, he thought, she was so devoted to him.

She had introduced Charles to French cuffs and cufflinks. The help at Ben Silver's now knew her by first name; she was one of their most enthusiastic customers. Charles had never seen or even heard of cufflinks before. As he sat at the table, he fiddled with one of them. It was a beautifully crafted thing. She had chosen an Irish harp design, green enamel set in gold. Her grandparents had come to Charleston from the Emerald Isle in the time of the Easter Rising in Dublin. There were many reversals of fortune for them. Sad to say, Charles knew a whole lot more about her people way back than his own.

Charles was looking at his face across the table reflected in the Chippendale mirror Hazel had found for the house in an antique store on King a few months ago. The mid-morning sun came through the bright dining room windows and seemed to light the crown of his head with the shimmer of burnished gold. Nadeen liked him to keep his hair neatly trimmed and groomed, and so he did. He had an agreement with a local barber who would come regularly to him. He'd left off wearing the ball cap because he didn't need it to hide tangled and disheveled locks any more. His barber was one of the new hair stylists who did both women and men. He'd fix all the women's and his too. It took him most of a day.

Shugg trotted into the dining room and sat at his master's feet. As Charlie looked at his face in the mirror, he heard Varzine tell Nadeen that the laundry was done. She was ready to help out there in the kitchen, but Nadeen sent her upstairs instead to tidy up and make the bed in the master bedroom. He heard Varzine's tread on the stair in the hall.

The house was one of those capacious classical revival beauties, at least one example of which was to be found in every small Lowcountry Carolina town. Kingstree in fact had a few, but this was the largest and most solidly built. They were all built around 1900 with scarce money that the owners had come by hard as a business or mill owner, a cotton or tobacco broker, or the like. Sovereign Bates, the builder of Nadeen and Charles's home, had been the owner and operator of a cotton and tobacco warehouse and the local cotton gin. He had owned a goodly portion of the town's real estate. He, or maybe his wife, liked the then fashionable classical style. The Bates children had now drifted away to larger venues and most of them had bigger fish to fry, or so they felt. Kingstree had gotten too small for them.

The Bates house had been kept in reasonably good repair by a series of owners by the time Charlie was born. Those were the days it didn't cost so much to make repairs and there was a sufficient supply of skilled carpenters, painters, and roofers around.

The house's last reincarnation was the not very successful Bates House Bed and Breakfast Inn. It just cost too much to operate and there weren't enough visitors to Kingstree. A cheap new chain motel had hurt business as well. Charlie purchased the house at a reasonable price. It had been on the slow real estate market for three years and the price was reduced several times. He gave the seller a little more than he asked. He thought it only fair not to take advantage of bad times.

Oddly enough, it wasn't the imposing columns on the house's front or its impressive size that attracted him. He was drawn instead to the scrolled ionic capitals of the columns and the large Palladian window in the projecting portico—names he didn't even yet know, but would in time. He thought the carefully detailed scrolls to be the most beautiful objects he'd ever seen. He'd only encountered them one other place, and that was on the old county court house. They spoke harmony and order to him, something young Charlie had rarely experienced until Miss Oma-Lynn took him in.

Charlie liked the house's big, quiet rooms made cool, dark, and comforting by their louver shutters and twelve foot high plaster walls. It was a solid house, constructed of brick two courses thick and overlaid with stucco. Outside noises did not penetrate within.

Today, he listened to the house sounds more acutely than usual, and took it all in. His little boy prattled to Hazel. He could just make that out. Nadeen sang. Varzine made the floors creak as she bustled about upstairs from room to room.

Charlie held the small frayed snapshot of his dad in his right hand. A corner was gone. The colour was now faded tobacco spit brown and blurred. In the picture, the father appeared to be the exact same age Charlie was then. He had on a ball cap worn at an angle just like Charlie used to do. The photo was snapped about the time he took off for parts unknown.

Charlie looked back and forth many times from mirror to photo and was struck by their resemblance. The two men could have been identical twins. For a moment, Charlie imitated his father's broad smile. The action was a little new to him. With the smile, the resemblance was even stronger. He had no doubt he was his father's son.

He looked deep and long. The photo against the cufflinks reflected in polished dark mahogany burned its image in his brain.

Charles Jr. began to cry upstairs. Feeding time again. Maybe a diaper change. Nadeen went up to assist Hazel and he was in the downstairs alone. The meaning of peace, he thought. I am blessed. In the quiet, he sat there not moving a muscle for another thirty minutes as if carved out of marble or a figure in bronze, his hand outstretched on the table with the photo in his open upturned palm, his back straight, not touching the back of the chair, and facing ahead. His eyes stared at his own image in the mirror hard and long. He liked the smoky oxidation of the antique glass. It allowed him to see past surfaces and look deep within. Its wavy old glass looked like the crystal glasses on the table before him and in the large sunny windows of the room.

In the stillness, he had made a solemn promise. He would find his dad. Charles Jr. might be given the chance of a grandfather he never had. Junior already had a dad.

The smell of pork ribs in the big oven woke him from his reverie. He could hear Varzine setting the kitchen table today, so as not to disturb him there in the dining room. He and Nadeen had started taking their dinners and suppers in the dining room, even though the table seated eighteen and they were only two. He could look into the future though and see sons and daughters lined up each side before him.

Nine

Search

He had so little of his father to go on—no information at all from his mama because she wouldn't allow his name to be spoken in the house. Then when she left, her mama Miss Oma-Lynn, would only shake her head and answer Charlie's questions with, "Honey, he was a bad lot." She wouldn't say another word beyond "You don't need to know." They never heard from his mother again. She didn't even come to the funeral when Miss Oma-Lynn died. She probably didn't know. Charlie pictured her as one of the homeless maybe camped under a bridge or highway overpass, somewhere vaguely out west. He hoped it was Southern California where the winters weren't so cold. She'd always hated the cold.

His father had come from Beaufort. That's about all he recollected from his grandma. From his sturdy look in the photo, he may have been a Parris Island Marine. He hadn't lived in Kingstree very long because Charlie couldn't find anybody there who remembered him or any of his kin. The telephone company had transferred him there after a big coastal storm. Charlie didn't know how he and his mama met. He'd always taken for granted they were married because he bore his name, but now he really didn't know. There were no records anywhere to this effect, and this was something he and Grandma would not have discussed.

Charlie was too smart to run through all of the new lottery cash. From the start, after paying several hundred million in taxes, purchase of the essentials of house and home, and the setting up of Nadeen's father and mother in safety in their home, he had 467 million left to invest. This he did in state municipal bonds. He reckoned he owned a goodly chunk of South Carolina thereby. He refused his agent's advice to diversify his portfolio. He wanted things simple. He didn't want to waste a lot of time keeping up with things. He'd done enough of that already in his life. The interest on the municipals brought him close to a tax-free twenty million each year. Some of what was left over at the end of the year, he'd plough back in to more bonds.

He'd be neither a spendthrift nor a miser either. He had a discreet financial agent in Columbia who took on the job of money management for a reasonable fee. A few percent of that amount was a reasonable salary in and of itself. Marc was an honor graduate in business from the local university. He had his diploma over his desk in the office high-rise downtown. Charlie every now and then glanced at it. It was like a token from a strange distant land. Out the 15th floor window, he could see the new burnished copper of the state house dome darkening and beginning to oxidize green. Charlie was good with figures and made it a point to take a few minutes to double check the tallies that Marc sent regularly. Although he figured Marc was honest, he felt he had no reason to trust this other world.

As Charlie saw it, he had the luxury of time, the greatest blessing of all. Marc said it was like retiring but Charles was doing it with his lifetime ahead. In his work, Marc declared that he'd seen dozens of men strive hard all their lives to put up a million dollars only either to die shortly after retiring or not have the time to make any long range plans or projects such as Charlie had. He said Charlie had youth and a youthful enthusiasm on his side, a rare thing for one so wealthy as he. He was happy for him. Marc himself worked long hours at the office, which cut into being home with his wife and children more than he wanted. He said it seemed he'd turned around and his children were nearly grown. He wasn't very close to them, but he'd made an effort for that to change. On top of his long hours, he had a five or six times a week commute, a chore that was getting very old. He never had time to enjoy the beach house on Sullivan's Island that his wife and children had insisted upon. His routine was grinding him down. He said he envied the fact that Charlie and his new family hardly ever had to be apart. Marc said that Charlie had the wherewithal to find his dad, if anyone could. Marc put him in touch with a private detective who had a good reputation in town.

Charlie hired the fellow and paid him his entire salary for six months to make this his sole priority. He had little more than Beaufort, the phone company, and the photo to go on. The detective said that other folks in his situation these days, believe it or not, had less.

So the search began. Charlie got a weekly report. The first information was that he wasn't a Marine. Parris Island had never heard of him. Neither had Beaufort. Second piece of information, Mack Gilyard may not be his name. If it was, he seemed to drop from the skies. Third, there was definitely no marriage certificate. Charlie now had to add the label bastard to his name. Fourth, he wasn't in jail or passed with that name through a funeral home or morgue. No one of his name or matching his image showed in records country wide. The detective would extend the search to Europe now. This was a very long shot because there appeared to be no passport for him in this name. It was looking more and more now like Gilyard wasn't his name in the first place, or if it was, it had now been changed. So the photo and Charlie's DNA was all they had to go on.

Charlie had only a single memory of him. A four-year-old's recollections are strange and unexplainably cryptic at best. All he remembered was that in being held close he felt the warmth and scratch of a wool garment against his cold cheek and the smell of what was likely a combination of beer, sweat, and after-shave.

Little to go on there. But time had not scaled that castle's keep. His memory's fortress had not been breached. The recollection was inviolate and as immediate as if it had occurred yesterday.

Charlie was now coming to understand that when a child, especially a boy, didn't have a father, the world, consciously or not, feels it can take advantage of him, and the lad could be made easy prey. Without a father, or even a brother, he is lessened and not given respect and regard. No one to protect; no one to redress wrongs; no one to stand up for him and defend. All his life Charlie had felt that vulnerability. He felt himself diminished and somehow beneath the world's regard. More and more to himself now, Charlie was gauging what had been his sensitivity. He wasn't a bad lad. His grandma had known it, and oddly enough, with hindsight, he realized that so had Miss Eustacia Carlisle.

Ten

Miss Eustacia

The house was a grey clapboard dwelling on a Kingstree side street in a modest neighborhood: 201 Live Oak Drive. The brass 201 on the letterbox at the door hadn't been polished in many a year. He'd located her address easily enough in the telephone book. He and Shugg went for a long walk and found the house. As he knocked he noticed the two large cushioned rockers on the front porch. One had a heavy yellow coat of tree pollen on the cushion and the other did not. He knocked several times and was about to leave when he heard a stirring inside. He recognized the tiny figure at once—as always, prim and proper, not a hair out of place. Her hair was completely grey now and she used a cane. It had taken a long time for her to get to the door. Her hair was the color of the moss that depended from the giant street trees.

She had on one of the trim grey dresses he remembered from school. In fact she was all grey like the house and its moss-shrouded yard on this overcast winter day. She looked up at him questioning, puzzled, wondering why this person had come, who this might be, what he had to sell. She got so few knocks at her door. The older sister who had lived with her had died two years ago, and she was now really alone.

Charlie paused to give her a little time to gather her wits, then gave her the hint of a smile. He asked her pardon for disturbing her, but felt he should look her up and say hello. Something in his voice kindled recollection. Her eyes narrowed and she recognized him. "Charlie Gilyard?" she asked somewhat tentatively. He nodded and smiled almost as broadly as his father in the tattered photo.

"Yes, ma'am, Miss Carlisle, present," he said.

She couldn't believe what a handsome young man he'd become. "I can't believe my eyes," she declared. "And so straight and tall." She asked him in. Charlie said sit and Shugg waited at the door. They sat in the dim parlor, he smelling the smell of all old houses through time. He watched the play of dust motes suspended in a solitary beam of light.

They talked at ease. He gave her the broad details of his recent life, his new wife and son. She hers. She'd never married. Her sister either. They lived out their lives together alone. Her pupils were her surrogate children; and with her retirement when rheumatoid arthritis nearly crippled her, she didn't have that any more. Her old principal and former fellow teachers never came around or called. It was as if she'd fallen off the edge of the world or into one of those dangerous uncovered wells at deserted old farm house sites in the country that curious explorers were always being warned about. One false step and you'd be no more and the world would never know. She felt she'd fallen in one of those wells. Now she sometimes wondered if she'd made any difference in the world, maybe even never had really existed at all.

When she lost her sister, she'd reached a new impasse. She said she'd now taken to reading all those books that she'd so loved and devoted her life to passing down to those like Charlie for half a century before. Charlie was a good and sympathetic listener. He'd learned that from being around Rodger when he was with Loutrell. So she poured all that out in a flood, and then catching herself, apologized. She'd not spoken to a single soul for the last three days or maybe more, she didn't know.

"That's okay," he assured her. "I want to know."

He told her how certain lines she'd spoken in class would come to him now and again. Seemed they came at just the right times when he needed them. It was very strange, he said. At that declaration, she was particularly pleased. She knew the comment was sincere. He said it was a gift she had given him. She answered him that the only thing we ever really have is what we give away.

After a long spell of quiet, he commented on all the books in the room. He'd never seen so many in a house before. "Old friends," she declared with a smile.

There were two tall antique mahogany breakfronts with tiny diamond shaped glass panes in the doors. Behind them he could see the glitter of gold on the leather spines. "The realms of gold," he thought out loud—another snatch of a line remembered from her class at school. He thought how no bank vault could hold so much gold. The grey room suddenly held its own golden light. There was light from within, as on a brilliant Easter sunrise. For a long time, the two said nothing, and there was dead quiet in the house as he took it all in. Even the dust motes stood still.

"Silent upon a peak in Darien," he said abruptly to both his and her surprise.

"And here it is," she answered, rising on her cane and walking carefully. He stood. She opened the case nearest them, drew out a volume, and brought it over to him. He focused on the breakfront's mahogany side columns, each with ionic scrolls for capitals, just like at his home and at the court house on the square.

"Chapman's translation of Homer," she said.

They sat again. He held the heavy leather volume on his knee as carefully as Charlie Jr. in the nursery. For a few minutes he turned the pages and didn't comprehend. He just knew the line from the poem and didn't make the connection to the book he held. He had no idea where or what was Darien.

With the intuition of a teacher of many years, she gauged his failure to understand, so recited the entire sonnet from a memory that had not in the least dimmed. Then she looked at him. "Chapman's Homer," she said again. She watched the light of recognition brighten his blue eyes.

From that charmed moment onward, they were to become fast friends.

He carefully returned the Homer for her to the bookcase; and as the great heavy doors of the breakfront closed over its treasures, their antique brass hinges made the creaking sound of the world turning on its axis once again. Though unseen, there was a third ancient companion in the room.

Eleven

The Sudden Scholar

His first assignment was to read Virgil. Miss Eustacia chose *The Æneid* in her favorite translation, the one she'd studied in college and which still had a prominent pride of place on her desk.

After hearing Charlie's story of his lost father and the search he and the detective had embarked upon, she wanted him to come across the moving passage of Æneas carrying his father on his back from burning Troy, carrying him on to the founding of Rome. Old lives end and new ones begin. She gave him the dog-eared copy. "Keep it," she said matter-of-factly, "And remember me."

By their next meeting the following week, Charlie had read the work and found *The Georgics* on his own. He was eager to ask questions and they talked several hours. "I have a lot to learn," he said. On that day of Chapman's Homer, Miss Eustacia had agreed to suggest weekly readings. Charlie was to set his own pace and not rush. They would not have a time table or schedule. They decided to meet twice a week. She'd get his reaction, answer questions, and fill in what blanks needed filling in.

Charlie was a God-send. She'd not wanted to leave teaching even with the growing bureaucracy and incessant paperwork and the growing push of politics in the schools. They seemed to be trying to take out all the pleasure and make it more difficult to do her job. Still, she missed it, even if the pupils were ill-prepared and most of them did not really want to be there.

The meetings with Charlie had become the one true luxury of her old age. She now had a student without the restraints and bondage of school. There were no tests, no attendance reports, no forms with little qualifying Xes and boxes to check or fill in, file, and turn in.

He was an eager reader, slow but careful in the ways that mattered. Sometimes he startled her with his freshness of insight and the feeling he brought to the work. She was a little surprised to find what a tender fellow he was. She could tell a lot about him from his responses to the works they read. She liked what she saw.

She had figured his first assignment right. The passage from Virgil resonated with him. So she gave him stories and poems of fathers, orphans, changelings, legitimate and illegitimate sons. He got a kick out of the life story of the foundling Tom Jones. She knew he would. In some ways, he'd already lived the story-line.

What Charlie needed, she soon reckoned correctly. He craved works that taught what she called the gentlemanly virtues. He needed to know honour and right behaviour, and their complicated and manifold ways. The popular world's surface never spoke of these things very much and seemed to value them even less. He'd come to the conclusion that what he was seeking so hard was more often than not scorned. Miss Eustacia knew that it was in her old friends on her shelves that the meanings he desired lived protected, undiminished, and unassailed.

He understood. One day he looked at the spines and said, "There they all are, looking at me and waiting." He had to pace himself. Like with all genuine and lasting friendships, things couldn't be rushed.

Miss Eustacia was shaping his character and bringing out the best in the man at just the right time he needed it. She found he already had the important traits in embryo and thus her work had fertile and receptive soil. What better way to guide than through her wise old friends. The enjoyment took double force because in many instances for her it was like meeting long-lost acquaintances once again. She realized now how much she had missed some of them. They were like her kin she'd lost touch with for awhile. The reunion was sweet.

Before the month was out, the tutorials had increased to three times a week. They had been moved to Charlie's quiet drawing room. He called for and carried her there, where she spent the day and had meals. Hazel had begun bringing them afternoon tea. The new physician Charlie had found for her was making progress in treating her arthritis and she did not always have to use her cane.

The progress in his books was remarkable. She had never seen such before. Certainly not in the experience of her college days and graduate school. Recently after he'd surprised her with insights she'd never had about certain chivalric lines from Sir Philip Sidney, she looked at him intently and remarked quietly half to herself, "Never was such a sudden scholar made."

Charlie smiled, gave that peculiar little laugh of his and said, "*Henry Five*, Act Two." They both chuckled at this. After a pause she said, "Really, Charles, though, Act One." They laughed again. Then Charlie declared in the exaggerated voice of an actor while standing and pointing to his chest, "As for me, we are blessed in the change!" Hazel brought in the tea to bring this mini-drama to a close. This time she had made scones and clotted cream.

The Henry plays were among his favorites now. She'd taught them to him in junior English class. They had taken partial root, but now he understood. To him, the plays were about the reversals in life, some owing to chance, but as often to choice, and usually most often in unpredictable combination. King Hal was his man. Life was about opposites, leniency and cruelty, duty and irresponsibility, taking and giving, dishonour and honour. The choice was Hal's.

So many people depended on him. So many depended on Charlie too. It was a new feeling for him. Maybe that was the catalyst, and demanding right thought and action. He wondered why the foolish world scorned the name gentleman these days?

One day Miss Eustacia told Charlie that each person could choose his literary fathers and mothers. Unlike his blood relations, he had the call and he should be certain to choose well.

As for Charlie and Miss Eustacia, they were now more than student and teacher, more than friends. He was the son she'd never had, and she was the mother he'd never really known.

When the second child was born, he and Nadeen were in a quandary for a name. This was serious. They floated all sorts of names. It was also a boy. Nadeen's father's name was unpronounceable and an alphabet of letters, so this wouldn't do. Charlie played with Virgil and Dante. He rejected Homer because there was already one with that name whom he didn't like much at the Feed and Seed Store. Æschylus, Sophocles, and Castiglione were out of the question. He'd never saddle anyone in Kingstree with one of these. Catullus and Apuleius were out as well. So were Wordsworth, Keats, and Coleridge. Only dogs were named Caesar. He never could spell Epictetus and Euripides. Byron might work, but there were already too many Byrons in town.

They had nearly settled on Horace when Nadeen asked why not Carlisle. Miss Eustacia was to stand in church as his godmother anyway. "Of course!" Charlie said.

And so it was done. The couple was correct in assuming that Miss Eustacia would take seriously to her grave the responsibility of that naming.

Twelve

A Chance Meeting

Loutrell was back in Kingstree now. He'd stayed in Pooler another seven weeks after he wrote his letter to Charles. His Uncle Rupert's patience finally wore out. In desperation, Rupert himself left home. He made a convenient undesired trip to a distant old friend in St. Augustine.

The day of Rupert's departure, it looked like Loutrell still wasn't going home, so when Loutrell went to the bait shop, Rupert packed Loutrell's clothes and fishing paraphernalia in his assorted canvas and paper shopping bags and one ancient battered suitcase and set them on the front porch with his fishing rods and tackle box and locked the door. A neighbour thought Rupert was fixing to have a yard sale and came over to enquire. Rupert had told Loutrell he was leaving, but Loutrell acted like he didn't hear him and went to the Bait and Tackle to swap fish tales. He'd made a little circle of friends there. You had to give him this—he wasn't stuck up.

Rupert in unaccustomed bluntness left a pointed note on the suitcase in a big scrawl. Just two words: *GO HOME*. He wanted to be nice and say that he'd enjoyed Loutrell's visit and come back soon and the standard things of well-meaning courtesy, but he didn't dare. As to his whereabouts in his travel to St. Augustine, he gave no details. Again, he didn't dare. He'd look up, and there would be Loutrell, talking a mile a minute as he came.

So here was Loutrell back at home in Kingstree at his old haunts again, telling everyone who would listen the trivia of his sojourn in Pooler, Georgia, in minutest detail.

Today he was crossing the square in front of the Williamsburg County Courthouse when he spotted Charlie-T. Charles was seated in a folding captain's chair with Shugg at his feet, head on paws, like her master enjoying the early December sun. Charlie was fiddling with a big sheet of paper on his knee.

Loutrell made a bee-line, and there followed the usual avalanche of words. Charles was courteous but kept on with his work. He was sketching the façade of the courthouse, now over a century and a half old. To tell the truth, he knew he wasn't much of an artist but was playing with the design, trying to bring back the original lines of the pediment before twentieth century renovation had changed them, and as Charles felt, not for the better. There was a picture of the old building hanging in the courthouse hall. He liked the original proportions, the order of the lines still present in the new, but purer before the embellishments.

The building spoke to him in ways he didn't understand, but the attraction was real. He was about to embark on a little building project at home and decided to rough out the plans. He probably didn't know it, but the courthouse was his closest local architectural link to classical Greece and Rome. Once again, as Miss Eustacia would say, he had *intuited* well. When she gave him a copy of William Faulkner's "Barn Burning" in which the character Sarty Snopes associates the columns of the local courthouse with Major DeSpain's great house and venerates them as symbols of order and fine ideals, Charles immediately grasped the implications. "Thanks, Miss Eustacia. I needed that," he said.

Loutrell noticed Charlie-T's clothes and the fine leather collar Shugg had on.

"All dressed up and noplace to go," he said. "You about to be tried?"

"No, Loutrell, just sketching," he answered. He was working at replacing in minute detail the fluting of the ionic capitals of the columns that the renovation had fancied up with frills.

"I bet you got a job to fix up something on that building. It needs new gutters, I know for a fact. You the one going to put them in?" Loutrell ventured, fishing for details.

"Nope." He was now inking in the delicate wrought iron turned scrolls of the handrails that had escaped the renovator's redesign.

"Uncle Rupert told me I ought to do something with my life except just scrounging around. Said a middle age man still had time if he didn't lack the inclination and imagination. I told him I was very satisfied just scrounging around and he told me that it was easy to be trash. You just didn't have to do anything and let everything slide. Instant trash. I thought that was a mite harsh. What he said made me a little hot at first, but I held my tongue as Uncle Rupert was putting supper on the table and I smelled cornbread. It got me to thinking though, but I couldn't for the life of me come up with a single thing I wanted to do and was good at. The collards was so good that night at supper that I told Rupert I might, if I had a little land, try to raise a few collards. Rupert said I had a lot of time on my hands and that would at least be a start. A person had to start somewhere. Charlie-T, you're a real young fellow. What you going to be?"

Charles looked up from the page and after some thought said, "A gentleman, Loutrell." He looked Loutrell in the eye in a way he'd not been accustomed to doing. Loutrell had to glance away. He'd never seen Charlie-T so serious before. He remembered how he'd usually look down when he talked and you looked at him. Wouldn't meet your eye. Like he'd done something to be ashamed of.

As a matter of fact, Charles had been giving that very question some thought of what he wanted to be for some time now, and that was the conclusion he'd come to. He was trying to figure out what the word gentleman meant. He'd reasoned that finding out what it was was the first step in living the word. Webster's just didn't cut it. He knew several folks, the one standing before him in fact, who didn't work for a living, who didn't engage in a menial occupation or in manual labour for gain, and what did noble birth have to do with it in a land without titles other than professional ones?

Webster's seemed to imply there could be no gentlemen in America. He had come to suspect Noah Webster anyway. Miss Eustacia helped him. She said Webster came from a place that didn't value gentlemen and scorned the word, was indeed about to make war on the word itself. Miss Eustacia said it was no wonder that their Charleston Library Society wouldn't allow Webster's dictionary in the building when she was growing up and stuck to Walker's London Dictionary. Charlie thought that maybe Webster, like himself, just didn't and couldn't understand. The main difference between them, as Charlie reasoned, was that he was trying to and wanting to understand, and Webster was rejecting the whole concept.

For so brief an answer to Loutrell, he knew it was a very complicated subject. It involved a world of things. He and Miss Eustacia had had long talks of this rising out of his readings. One of his favourites was now Sir Philip Sidney. Charles had learned much from him. Still two of his grandmother's sayings that she'd learned from her father had not been contradicted by what he'd read. Miss Oma-Lynn had often told him, "Quality isn't *is*, it's *does*" and "Success isn't the *how much* of achievement but the *how*." Miss Eustacia thought that these were wise observations. All they'd read, in fact, had in some ways played variations on these themes.

Last week, seeing how Charles had taken to Sidney, Wyatt, and Surrey in the past month, she'd given him one of their sources, a good translation of *The Book of the Courtier*. He'd read it straight through. It made such good sense to him and went a long way in answering the question that had been dogging his mind.

"I'll bet King Hal read this book," he told Miss Eustacia. "No doubt," she answered. "His whole world did."

They discussed why the gentleman wasn't much in fashion anymore, and came to the conclusion that folks didn't have the time and if they did, it didn't pay. It also implied gradations and levels in a world that was obsessed with everybody and everything being equal and the same.

But here was Loutrell, Charles thought. He had as much time as himself, and likely a lot more, because Charles was spending a good bit of it with his boy and Nadeen.

Well, Charles's answer was lost on Loutrell. No matter. He wasn't really listening anyway. He'd spotted one of his fishing buddies going into the P.O. "The Fisher King on the canal," Charles thought as he watched Loutrell bound across the square. "Still fishing by the slimey canal as his kingdom falls apart."

He was a little relieved at Loutrell's going. He looked at Shugg sleeping at his feet, her head still on her paws. Charlie tried to remove a smudge his thumb had made on his drawing at the point of the courthouse portico while, distracted for a moment, he'd listened to Loutrell.

Thirteen

The Realms of Gold

The Bates great house had a capacious eight-acre back green, an unheard of luxury in even a small Southern town. In deciding to buy the property, Charlie had felt that for one thing, Shugg would have a bigger place to roam, chase squirrels, and be a normal dog. After a trip to England, Mrs Sovereign Bates had had the idea that she wanted to play croquet, and have a clay tennis court. She thus had a croquet field and two clay courts installed. With the passage of a century now, they had grown up into a tangle of privet, cat brier, wisteria, and weeds. The Bates family also had the area's first swimming pool. The bed and breakfast owner who was something of a Lowcountry botanist and plant collector, converted it into an ornamental water-lily and pitcher-plant bog.

Charles had the swimming pool and tennis court area reclaimed as the site for one of the two buildings he had gotten a crew out of Charleston to build. They specialized in historic properties and had the reputation of being among the best in the country. This new project was the reason he was sketching the court house last week.

The first structure located adjacent to the guest house where Hazel stayed, was to be a tidy suite of small rooms for Miss Eustacia. Charlie knew that with no family at all, when she needed care, it would be up to him. The alternative would be a nursing home. The house he was building would already be useful now too. Miss Eustacia could join them for formal suppers in their big, mostly empty dining room and stay there without having to go home. When their reading and discussing would run long, she could stay over if she wanted to.

He designed the rooms with her declining mobility in mind. Kitchen, bathroom, bedroom, and parlour were all on one level. There were no steps, not even door thresholds. Everything was maneuverable if a wheel chair had to be used.

As for her house on Live Oak Drive, Charlie had a crew over last month to scrape and paint. Nadeen and Miss Eustacia chose a sunny cream yellow instead of grey. Charlie had their yard man go over once a month to tidy the yard. This was a great relief to Miss Eustacia. Even though she tried to put such to the back of her mind, and deal with problems as they occurred, the worries always shadowed her mind. She didn't like the place to look shabby.

Getting old wasn't good. It's certainly not for sissies, she said. This living life one day at a time was a necessity she had to accept, but still didn't like.

Charles kept her new house design simple. Its object was for the building to fit in. He was proud that it complemented the guest house it was to sit next to. Varzine and Hazel recommended a trellised breezeway that would connect the two. They both thought the world of Miss Eustacia. Hazel already had her ideas about what climbing old garden roses she'd get to cover the breezeway. She was something of a rosarian when she had time. She told Nadeen that "Sombreuil," "Cloth of Gold," and "Gloire de Dijon" were musts and knew a Charleston nursery that stocked them.

For Charles, his other project would be a dream come true. With the bulk of the year's interest from his investments, he would build a separate little temple of a building for his and his family's personal library. That was the main reason he was sketching the courthouse. It would sit comfortably sheltered and cooled by a giant moss-draped live oak where the pool and tennis courts had been. Charlie liked this tree best of all on the grounds for its shape and the veritable garden of thick emerald green moss and resurrection fern growing on its gnarled limbs.

At first he'd planned to convert one of the 25 by 25 foot rooms in the house for the library, but had nixed the idea when he thought of the racket of daily activity and active children. It was to be a quiet place for contemplation. He would also want to share it, and share it with some folks he might not want in the privacy of his home. A library in the house would be more exclusive than he wanted it to be. He also wanted room to set out a dozen or so comfortable straight chairs in addition to the leather wing chairs. He might have some sort of talks or readings for some in the community. What he'd found was too good not to share.

Noblessse oblige. He'd learned those words just recently. The only other French he knew was *le chevalier sans peur et sans raproche*, the sobriquet of another of his recently made friends the Chevalier Bayard met in an antique biography. He got the pronunciation down reasonably well with Miss Carlisle's aid.

Miss Eustacia had given him her father's copy of a Charleston published biography of the good French knight written by one of her family's friends during the palmy days—an author named Simms. He'd never heard of him, but Miss Eustacia said there was a bust of him at White Point Gardens in Charleston. Charles had never seen it. He vowed he'd take Jr. there one day, because he liked this book a lot.

In its pages, he found answers to some of the questions on his mind these days. It was Miss Eustacia's own father's. What a treasure of a gift. He looked at the beautiful handwritten script on the creamy vellum. His name was there. It had been his father's before him. The elder Carlisle had signed and dated it 1861 under a pasted library plate with the Carlisle name and an etching of a three-story house that must have been their own. Miss Eustacia said it was their townhouse on Legare. The writing looked like calligraphy to Charles. He wondered about a time that could take so much pride and care in handwriting. The signatures were a little history in themselves. He looked at them long, and finally ran his fingers over them caressing. The ink had not faded. The creamy vellum was unspotted. The watered marbleized endpapers looked like channeled rivulets of bright and glistening tears the sun was shining through and making into rainbows.

The volume's gold stamping on royal blue made it another citizen in the realms of gold, and written and published, then owned, by Miss Eustacia's people, and through Miss Eustacia, one of his family too.

At the announcement of the library project, Hazel and Varzine had gone into a frenzy of shopping, particularly Hazel in the antique stores on King. She had already located a gentleman's period Sheraton partner's desk to sit in the middle of the room. Last week, she found two treasures, matching fifteen foot long glass-paned English breakfronts to complement the built in, leather- and felt-lined library shelves which Charles had planned for two of the walls. Charles made a few references to Hazel's "shopaholism," shook his head, and smiled. She knew he was both amused and pleased at the same time.

Miss Eustacia was happy that Charles showed unbridled excitement for this project. She'd never seen him that way before. There was now never any glancing down at his feet. His smiles were not fleeting and wistful, but real. At times, they were broad. For the first time, she noticed how perfectly regular his teeth were. She commented to herself that he had a lovely smile and how completely until now, all that had been hidden away.

She decided that when the library was completed, she'd give him her books, many collected by her grandfathers Carlisle and Sass and great-grandfathers Smythe and McCord before. Some had been saved from the fires and lootings of war to be part of the large

Augustine Smythe personal library on Legare, in the house across from her grandfather Carlisle. Most of these had been collected by Smythe's Lowcountry in-laws, David and Louisa McCord. They had come down to Eustacia from her and their O'Neill kin on Legare.

She recollected from her granny Sass how on her father's Black River plantation in 1865 when everything was going to smash and the great house sat empty, former slaves at the encouragement of the blue-coated invaders, stripped the house of everything they could use and destroyed the rest. Great Grandpa Sass's carefully kept plantation records, letters, colonial land grants, and other documents going back to the 1600s were strewn a foot deep on the library floor by those intent on finding a banknote or coin. The books were tumbled from the shelves with inexplicable vengeance. Many of the volumes were taken outside and ripped apart to form a circle around the house. Later, one of those who could not read explained that the reason they had done so was because the white man's power over him had come from the magic in the books. Destroy the books, and you destroy the power. It was as simple as that. The circle of rain-washed volumes, leather bindings curling as they dried in the spring sun, was a protection like a fort against his masters' former power.

All the books that were not ruined beyond repair were gathered up and taken to their home in Charleston. Although the books were now very valuable objects of commerce, just another commodity in the modern world, the family had not sold them off, even when there was little money for bread. Once Colonel Sass had taken his treasured copy of Sir Walter Scott's Peveril to the used bookseller on King and came home with a cut of meat for their Christmas dinner. He made light of the irony of transforming a pompous, dry fellow like Peveril into a juicy meal. The next week Sir Walter's Abbot was resurrected into a leg of lamb, but the empty space which the volumes left on the shelves accused him. He declared, "That bookshelf is a grinning mouth, with black holes where teeth had been," and he never went that route again. He would not see romantic inspiration lost to commerce, or at least it would be the last to go before breath itself. Books were like friends and family, read, and revisited, and quoted as comfort and wisdom.

The dark years had taken most every material thing from them, including the house on Legare, the physical library room on the third floor itself, the furniture exchanged for food, but the books had been saved. As Miss Eustacia strolled the narrow byways of Charleston as a child, it was like walking the streets of Pompeii. She had the feeling that this had been the site of a profound calamity. She was grateful that at least out of the ruins, their books had been saved, and her people's access to them. For her, it was their connection to the civilised things that mattered in the world.

Miss Eustacia had not had the money to add many volumes of their quality to the library, but the few that she had bought were well chosen and rare. She and her sister had not liked to think what would happen to the volumes when they were dead. Miss Eustacia thought that if her sister had known Charlie's plans, she would have been pleased. Miss Eustacia was more than pleased. She was relieved.It had been a very close call. It was like that in their broken world, had been like that for a century and half. If at all, things survived by the skin of the teeth. She recollected Sir Alister Clark's declaration that oftentimes civilisation had itself only survived by the skin of its teeth. And yet it had, in miraculous, unpredictable ways. That's where faith came in.

As she looked back and forth from her old friends behind their diamond panes, to the new gilt-framed photograph of a smiling golden-haired Charlie holding his son, she was indeed very relieved.

Fourteen

Portable Property

Hazel was excited. She'd found two matching wing chairs for the library, "period eighteenth century antiques in good condition and in real old leather!" she exclaimed. They had just come on a container crate through the port of Charleston from one of the great English country houses. She had been the first to see them in the shop on King. Shugg could be allowed on them if she behaved. This time her preference for floral chintz took a backseat. She'd also located a set of twelve period Chippendale straight chairs from a bankrupt Philadelphia estate. Unheard of in that number, Sotheby's said. Luckily, Charlie had ample temporary storage space in the room over the 1930's garage where Mr. Bates' chauffeur had lived.

This outbuilding had three folding doors for the Bates vehicles acquired at the height of their influence in town. One was a cream colored roadster with soft green leather upholstery that would have made Jay Gatsby jealous. A sedate black touring car sat in another bay under a dusty car cover deteriorated with age. The garage was screened discretely by giant old alba plena *Camellia japonicas* within proximity to the house's port-cochère.

The chauffeur's room was now full to the ceiling with furniture waiting for the library. Charlie looked ahead to the time when the chauffeur's room was cleared, renovated, and furnished. He figured he could give employment as a driver to some worthy book-loving lad who'd need the job. Nadeen, Miss Eustacia, Varzine, and Hazel would already find him handy, and sometimes so might he. He'd never found driving the thrill it was to all his peers of both sexes, rich and poor, in high school. Nadeen, in fact, didn't have much confidence in him behind the wheel. She declared he looked at everything but the road. Varzine said she was going to get him a bumper sticker reading **CAUTION. I BRAKE FOR TREES.** Charlie said he wouldn't care. Maybe it would start a trend.

The passion for trees was somewhat new to him, but he had guidebooks that opened the great arboreal world. Nadeen declared to Miss Eustacia that Charlie was interested in everything, to which she replied that this was as it should be.

In her collection of books was another treasured volume written and published in Charleston during war times by one of her kin: *Forest Resources of the South*. The author was her great grandfather's cousin Frances Porcher. Cousin Frances had signed it to her grandfather with the admonition to keep his powder dry and hide his silver and old Madeira. The work gave the natural world's replacements for all the things being denied the South with the cruel blockade. For Charlie's 26th birthday, she wrapped it in bright blue and green, put a silver ribbon on it and presented it to him.

Charlie continued to smile at Hazel's active purchasing and encouraged her from time to time with that little laugh of his. "As if she needed encouragement," Nadeen said.

Charlie's funny little laugh was enough, no words needed, and she understood. Charlie had taken up one of Miss Eustacia's Dickens novels and liked the fatherly advice of one of his characters to get portable property.

"Get portable property" became Charlie's humorous little saying with which he'd season any discussion of household finances. The portable property wouldn't be just anything of monetary value though. A newly-learned Latin word *virtù* governed the choice. Objects of *virtù*, they should be. He and Miss Eustacia talked. She was not surprised to find Charlie knew exactly what the word meant, and much better than a dictionary could explain. "Getting for all the right reasons, Charlie," she said, and he was satisfied.

Miss Eustacia was helping Charlie fill the gaps in the library collection. There were certain books she'd always wanted and knew Charlie should read. The librarian in Kingstree helped Hazel and Miss Eustacia work through the internet to get rare editions from booksellers throughout the world. The librarian declared to Hazel that Mr Gilyard must be a sybarite. He'd specified he would not purchase any newly bound volumes. He wanted the sumptuous original leather, hand-tooling, and gilt edges. He was even making a little collection of books whose fore-edges had miniature landscape scenes. He loved marbleized endpapers, in fact, anything hand made.

Nadeen would sometimes find Charlie seated in the drawing room, rubbing lanolin leather cream into centuries old bindings, just for the feel of leather at his finger tips and palms. A sybarite indeed, he now knew and lived the meaning of the word.

When Hazel looked up the meaning of sybarite, she wholeheartedly agreed, and was a bit relieved. At first, she thought it might be an ugly word. She had heard the rumors of her boss's early years with activities that went beyond the usual wild oats.

So portable property it would be. She remarked to Varzine, "God, but I love this job!" Her pride in Charlie and the place grew with each day. They were building something special here, and she had a part in it. Charlie saw her pride and approved. It was all good. He was learning that proper loyalty worked both ways and portable property could be some of the cement to bind, and without such binding, what good would it be anyway and just how long would it last? In important ways, they all had co-ownership.

Fifteen

Loutrell and The Jalapeño

Loutrell picked Rodger up at the Piggly Wiggly on the way to Lake Moultrie. They'd be getting a late start today. Loutrell said it was Rodger's fault, as it truthfully usually always was. They were so late, in fact, that they got hungry on the way. Loutrell had forgotten and left their lunch on the kitchen table back home. This just wasn't his day.

The only restaurant open on the route to the lake was this new El Habanero, catering to the migrants doing field work in the fields around St. Matthews. Rodger and Loutrell hadn't ever eaten at a Mexican restaurant before, but after Loutrell had met Miss Georgia Latina he'd had a hankering to try one. They both wondered what *Ha-ba-ner-o* meant.

They soon found out. Hot, hot, hot! Hot-to-mighty hot!. "Whew!" Rodger breathed. "Hot as the hinges of hell." Sweat broke out on their brows. The flaming orange and red picture of the bull aiming its horns at the matador's shiney red tight silks in a red bull ring surrounded by red faces suggested the flames of hell and about summed it all up. Loutrell's sun-tanned face turned pale and made him look a real gringo. Rodger's white forehead turned scarlet like the faces in the mural.

"Whoo-ee!" Rodger gasped, but they were hungry and kept on eating. "Put some of this green stuff on it. It's green; maybe it'll cool it off," Rodger advised as he poured half the dish of jalapeno on his food.

"Ow-wee. Drink water," Loutrell said, gulping. "This green stuff made it worse!" The water did too.

Loutrell was now struggling for air. He was silent for the first time in his life.

After some time the waiter came back and apologized. Between them, Rodger and Loutrell could piece together some of what he said. Seems the cook had gotten into the tequila and put all the three kinds of hot peppers for the whole restaurant that day into the sauce for their two meals.

Rodger had wondered why the beef burrito was grass green, but he didn't have experience enough to question. He really didn't know that it shouldn't be. The green juice of jalapenos and a whole king size bottle of habanero sauce even bled into the dough and made it green too. They had wondered why there wasn't meat, but figured this must be the Mexican way. "Cook must be one of them foreign vegetarians," Loutrell concluded.

The two stared at each other with teary eyes when they were through. Neither had ever left anything on his plate before, and they weren't going to start today, especially when they had to pay for the food. Good money was too hard to come by to waste.

They were sweaty and looked wilted and exhausted as if they'd run a long race. Loutrell was already anticipating tomorrow with fear and trepidation. "Better put the toilet paper in the freezer when we get home," he said. Rodger assented but after a moment of serious quiet, replied, "Reckon I'll be using the creek to keep from setting fire to the woods."

They got on their way, caught some fish, and on their return, looked at the flashing red **El Habanero** sign with new-found wisdom and their one Mexican word. *Habanero—Pepper*, they said in unison. The blinking neon effigy of a red pepper seemed to smoke and sprout horns and a forked tail. *Habanero—Pepper* they gasped once again as the blinking restaurant sign showed in the truck's rear view. With these fellows, this was learning the hard but only way.

Sixteen

Swift Transitions

As Charles held his new born second son, little Carlisle Gilyard, the words to Miss Oma-Lynn's favorite gospel hymn came into his mind and dominated his afternoon. She sang it a lot and in his memory he could hear her sweet refrain: *Life is filled with swift transitions. Hold to God's unchanging hand.*

In the moment now, he held Carlisle's wrinkled red fingers and reckoned that if the little boy was aware of his father's hand holding his, to him the hand must appear to be God's. That sobered his exhilaration. He thought about the word *unchanging*. That was solely the Creator's property, and not portable at all.

Nadeen was sleeping. It had been a difficult birth. Labor had to be induced and Carlisle had to be taken by c-section. He was a big past-due child, a strapping healthy boy, and Nadeen was petite. In centuries past, she would likely have died, and maybe the baby as well.

Miss Eustacia had been teaching Charlie the word *mutability*. It seemed to be one of the favourite themes of the works he'd been reading now for a year. "A crash course in transience," she said and smiled. She explained that the word and its meaning were doubly important back then in the old days to prepare the folks in those times. She said they had such an uncertain world, in some ways even more uncertain than theirs, so that it was much on the poets' minds. More children died than lived to maturity and life expectancy was such that if she'd been living in those times, she would now be living for two. Charlie himself wouldn't even have another decade left in order to hit the mean.

Death was always at the elbow. No wonder skulls were carved on the grey slate markers at the oldest cemeteries in their town. They appeared more often than the winged faces of cherubs or crowns. Yes, the empty hour glass, it was there too—incised by the hand of the skilled stenciller whose own bones lay nearby.

Charlie's Southern world understood mutability. He still knew only a little of the South's history, learned only a bit here and there from what people said. It was a knowledge picked up mostly in snatches and from osmosis. It was implicit in their individual family histories taken collectively, passed on from the older generation to the new.

Just the other week, Charlie had taken the afternoon to read his newly-acquired volume of Robert Burns. The famous poem about the plans of mice and men ganging oft awry gave him pause. He supposed he was like the wee mouse beastie building his nest. Miss Eustacia's house was nearing completion. His library was begun. He'd turned away one builder and now had one who understood his ideas and had the skill to match. He had a new son.

Better not tempt God. He'd slow down on plans for a while. He learned from his reading that he better not presume. And he had a baby to devote time to.

The leather binding of the Burns volume, now two and a half centuries old, had a beautiful hand-tooled gold design on its red morocco covers, the classical Greek key interlaced with an ivy twine that Miss Eustacia called filigree. Many hands had made it and many hands had taken care of it. How new and fresh the designs looked. The rare book dealer had called the volume in dealer-talk *pristine*. Charlie marveled that at least six generations had been its good caretakers. All it would have required was one careless owner, a hurricane, or invader's torch, and he would not now be holding it in his hands. All that procession of careful folks was gone to their graves and outside man's memory. Only two of their names remained, written in fading ink on the browning flyleaves. The leather hadn't so much as cracked at the book's hinges, and yet most of the owners were anonymous dust under foot in places unknown.

He and Miss Eustacia celebrated the arrival of the book by special post with stem glasses of Madeira from an antique cut-glass decanter Hazel had recently brought in. Miss Eustacia had to help him with Burns's Scots dialect. It came easy enough to her because her people were of Scottish descent. Her great great grandfather had left Charleston to study in Edinburgh, and her father had wanted to send her for a semester to St Andrews. This hadn't happened though. Such were his plans, but all his attempts to get the wherewithal fell through. Still, she studied the literary works of the native heath, more for his sake than hers. She knew her Walter Scott, the Ettrick Shepherd, Shenstone, and Burns. They were very distant relatives of Sir Thomas Carlyle. Certain lines of *Sartor Resartus* were everyday sayings in her family.

Her father had told her much of the old days from stories which his grandfather and father had told him. In the old days they'd not have had to worry about the means for the important things. The family and their society had valued education and intellectual endeavour as much as any material things. For education, many sacrifices were made. And the best of that was to be had in Cambridge and Leipzig, Göttingen, Heidelberg, and Berlin.

Over their second glass of Madeira, this time an old family-descended Malmsey that Miss Eustacia had been saving for an occasion like this, she told Charlie the origin of her given name. Her father was a great reader of the novelist Thomas Hardy. The pessimism of Hardy's works seemed to match his city's gloom at the time. When he was a lad, grass grew in Charleston's thoroughfares and the buildings were unpainted and forlorn. Porches rotted, sagged, and fell awry. Families retreated into their tall rooms with shutters seldom open to the sun. In some of the houses, even certain floors of their ancestral halls were shut and never entered by any one. In the delicately carved cornices outside, decay had set in. She was named for Hardy's tragic heroine Eustacia Vye. Her sister was named Tess, and their ill-fated little brother who died young was named Jude. When Charlie read the works from which these names came, he quickly understood so much about the world into which she was born. In many ways, it was his own world too and of many in the town. They still lived in the dark shadow of deprivation caused by war.

The old bottle of Madeira led Eustacia to tell Charlie how hidden bottles of this preferred drink of the flush times before the war had gotten several families whom her father knew through the raven days after the war. Bottles of these families' choice Madeira that survived looting were auctioned off in the wealthy cities of the North and this paid many a bill. They put food on the table of some, her own family included. Her grandfather had told her mother to hide the best bottles because they might be needed for a bank account after the war, and he was right. She said the Charleston Jockey Club, of which her grandfather was an officer, had hidden their large stock of over 2000 bottles and sold them off for several decades after the war to keep families from feeling the pinch of hunger. She said it was a time of houseless heads, headless houses, and pinched bellies.

That same week when Eustacia told him about Madeira, Charlie ordered a significant number of old bottles of Port and fifty cases of the best aged fifteen year reserve Broadbent Malmsey Madeira to stock a now completed wine room. His inventory was growing and he was learning from Eustacia the fine points of wine appreciation. He said to himself that learning Madeira and sharing the knowledge with others was at least a gesture at getting back a bit of the culture that had been their heritage and should have been their birthright. He had already become fond of drinking it at table, as the folks of the old times did. Eustacia said it was the tea of the old days. Juleps were not anywhere nearly as popular. In fact, she said their family felt juleps to be a newcomer and somewhat common next to Malmsey. You certainly couldn't drink them at dinner. They were much too sweet.

From Miss Eustacia's stories, Charlie realised now what swift transitions all their people had suffered, and just how truly swift those transitions had been. Ashes and smoke, mounds of crumbled moss-covered old brick, solitary house chimneys, deserted farms, etched skulls, overgrown tangled gardens, and hour glasses and cherubs were strung jumbled in a long continuous chain in his tired brain. He expected that it was holding God's hand that had gotten these people through. It was certainly so for Miss Oma-Lynn.

Little Carlisle still had a tight hold on his forefinger. Quite a grip. Charlie wiggled it loose and handed him back to the nurse. Nadeen was still asleep. He suddenly felt the exhaustion of no rest now for two days. He had been with Nadeen both night and day. He'd been running on adrenalin the last twenty-four hours. The colour of his cheeks rose and they burned. He hoped it wasn't a fever coming on. The nurse told him to get some sleep in the little narrow bed they'd had wheeled into Nadeen's room for him. The nurse commented that he should rest because it would be a shame to lose the daddy, after the mamma and baby had come through.

The minute his head touched the pillow, he was asleep. He'd not realised how exhausted he was. His sleep was so deep he couldn't even remember his dreams.

Seventeen

Taking Stock

Nadeen was fully recovered now. Good thing; she and Hazel had their hands full. At breakfast one morning when Charlie and she were alone, he brought up the tender question of the bedroom.

With her difficult delivery and her Catholic strictness on birth control, if they didn't want more babies right away, he told her he'd have to do his best to abstain. That's all he could figure; it was a dilemma for him. She quickly put an end to that possibility. She wanted more children. Her next birth would probably be easier, the doctor explained. In making the decision, she didn't care. She especially wanted a daughter. So did Varzine. Nadeen came from a large and close family before it was fractured by war. Charlie was greatly relieved.

Nadeen was pleased that Charlie was keen on the bedroom. In the absence of experience and parental guidance, they had done what came naturally. Charlie had no problems there. The curse of soaring testosterone levels as a young fellow that had given him such problems in that old life, was now a blessing. No men's clinic for him. No little blue pill.

They were both modest. He'd draw the heavy tapestry curtains on the massive four poster bed. In the big high-ceilinged master bedroom, this made a small place just their own. With the world walled out and out of mind, they could concentrate their intentions.

In the spring, she found she was expecting their third child. During the long winter nights, their tapestry curtains were drawn more often than left open. They both liked to sleep with them that way. Hazel saw to it that they always had the finest and most comfortable silk bed clothes and linens that money could buy. She had to persuade him to silk pajamas, but after one night, he was convinced. She'd stocked his closet with several robes. Naden had the sheerest silk and hand-made Irish lace. Nadeen had innate good taste which Charlie soon learned to see and appreciate.

Nadeen was thankful that Charlie was totally devoted to her. He had his projects during the day, but also took up much time with Junior and Lisle. After supper with her and the boys, the four were together until bedtime, when Hazel came on the scene scolding, directing, talking baby talk to the lads, and in general managing in her efficient way.

Hazel slept with the children in the nursery which was at the other end of the house from the master bedroom. She respected their privacy. She was particularly scrupulous in this. So far there had been no grave calamity to cause her to knock on their bedroom door.

Charlie's library was nearly complete. While he looked from the dining room windows at the workers busy at their jobs, he was taking stock of himself. Varzine had cleared his and Nadeen's dishes and Hazel had the boys. Nadeen was off to the Fresh Market in town. She had a keen craving for a particular mushroom she'd loved as a child. This gave him the time for unhurried thinking, which was becoming more and more his way.

He had his now well-worn Shakespeare beside him at the table. As was often the case, it was open to *Henry V*. His man Hal in his youth had been a rowdy one, had been unkindly but accurately dubbed *pantler* and *bread-chipper*, a fellow who'd at best be able to govern some fine lord's pantry. Charlie chuckled as he reckoned that in his youth he'd outdone Prince Hal's pantler and bread-chipper. Then there was Harfleur, Agincourt, his loving Kate, and a son. Dead from dysentery at the age of thirty-three. Charlie concluded that maybe he wasn't doing as much as he should, but was doing tolerably well, considering how far he'd had to come and so quickly. Hal had been born the king's eldest son, with father and loving brothers, a prince of power no less, with the world at his feet. His father had loved him and bequeathed him a crown and a realm. Charlie had a torn yellowing photo and not even memories.

Charlie didn't have a military bone in his body and would not go the route of Agincourt and of Hal's happy few and his band of brothers. He hoped that outside war, there were honour and bravery daily, hourly, in his routine. The concepts quietly seeded the minutia of his life. As in the lives of many good people, it was bravery usually unremarked by anyone, or even thought of..

He closed the big book at his elbow as a ray of April sun fell on his head and the yellow down on his hand. The sun felt good on them, though his hand held no sceptre or his head had no crown.

Eighteen

Doge

Yesterday Charlie went out to the building site, Shugg at his heels. He thanked the men for their work. There was a young fellow of about nineteen who reminded Charlie of himself at that age. He usually sat quietly on the edge of things. His name was Carlton. He didn't have a nickname like the rest of the men.

A careful worker, he was one of the first and most active men on the job. From the deference he paid everyone, you could tell he was at the bottom of the pecking order there. No one mistreated him, but the men's attitude showed that they didn't take him too seriously. He was more than ten to twenty years younger and green. If any of them needed a gopher task done, he was the one they called upon. He complied with energy and didn't seem to mind. Charlie never heard him curse or complain. He walked with a purposeful stride.

Charlie planned to have a sit-down talk with him in a few days. Until then, he'd watch from his window and draw his conclusions from what he'd seen. If he wasn't mistaken, Carlton seemed to be the kind of fellow he'd like to help in some way.

As for the rest of the men, he knew they needed the work he was supplying them in this time of serious slump in the building trade. Cash was tight and no one was taking any risks. He picked up details of their lives from snatches of conversation he overheard and from details Varzine and Hazel in some cases could fill in.

One, Hazel's distant cousin, had six children to feed and his wife had just been diagnosed with leukemia. Another was supporting his elderly mother and a sister whose husband had been killed in a car wreck last year. Sis needed his help until she could get back on her feet. The couple had just had their first child before the accident, his first nephew. Another's wife had just run off with the church choir director. She took his car and the portable property, but left three children to feed and get through school. They had outstanding medical bills and she'd managed to max out three credit cards before she'd cleared out. He owed close to thirty thousand dollars on them. The men joked that she'd just been taking her cue from Congress in spending and leaving others to pay. He hadn't been unmanned by the situation, however, and was already dating a smart and knock-out beautiful young woman. The men joked that at least his wife hadn't taken his balls. "Pretty much everything else though," he replied, "And probably would have had them too if they hadn't not been worth a dollar and hadn't been so securely attached."

About half the crew was made up of Spanish-speaking men homesick for their families back home. Lord knows what stories of hardship and tragedies they could tell. These outsiders ate their lunches to themselves—lots of tropical juices, canned tins of pineapple, and mangoes, guavas, and strange fruits Charlie couldn't name. Cans of Vienna sausages he knew from experience. Their language was unintelligible to Charlie. They spoke intently and sometimes with great peals of laughter at something someone must have said. Maybe a joke from some far distant land.

They had a kind of foreman who could speak both languages and was the go between. Carlton got along with these men and had picked up enough of their language to converse. He seemed to have something in common with them. Charlie reflected that they were getting to work earlier than the rest, working extra hard, and having natural good manners. He learned that these foreign men were sending every penny of their wages they could spare to families back home and hoped one day they'd be able to make enough money to return.

The young ones especially were homesick. One, who looked no more than fifteen, a delicate young fellow with artist's hands, did all the tiny paint trim work. Charlie noticed how sad he looked. One day he and Carlton were finishing a chore by the big rose bush at the side of the site. It was winter but there were still a few sheltered pink blooms. The lad looked at Carlton with a little smile, cupped one of the pale blossoms in his hand, and said "Rose." Carlton figured this was one of the few English words he knew. It was the only one he'd heard him say. Carlton would bring him a little gift from time to time. The ones he seemed to like best were a used garden book of flowers and a little guide book of Renaissance art in Rome.

Charlie watched this microcosm of human nature mostly from afar. He was glad he could afford to hire them and was paying them well. He made certain that his munificence trickled down even to the lowest on the ladder. He knew he was making a difference in their lives. The library of things that mattered that he was building should not be built on anything less. Wouldn't the task be pointless otherwise? Wouldn't the very foundations of the structure crack and crumble?

The next few mornings that Charlie watched the crew, Carlton was the first on the job, even before the foreigners. Carlton sat on the jobsite or stood around with his hands warming in his pockets waiting for orders until the foreman arrived. Others coming in to the job, even the foreigners in their beat-up old vans, stayed in their vehicles with engines idling, truck heaters heating, eating their fast food breakfasts, some already smoking, or drinking coffee from their thermoses. Winter was setting in early this year.

Carlton's breath was white in the cold. Already they'd had several hard freezes and had to wait until it warmed sufficiently, to mix mortar for the bricks, the men's least favourite job.

These past days, Carlton and the young Guatemalan lad had the mortar mixing detail. They never got behind and this was due to Carlton's energy and strength, for he was a strapping young man even if he didn't bow himself up and swagger his strength around. Carlton and the delicate boy looked a mismatched pair. Charlie noticed that Carlton didn't smoke or chew. The locals took their dinner hours at fast-foods in town. Carlton brought his in a used plastic bread bag. The foreigners brought coolers and paired off in little groups. Carlton sometimes sat alone. Charlie noticed that his flannel shirts were the worse for wear, and this week he'd worn the same one for three days. His jeans were clean but torn. His Red Man boots were showing wear. Charlie had worn Red Man boots too when he could get them only a few years ago.

One day when Carlton was eating his sandwich alone, Charlie, Shugg as usual at his heels, took him a piece of Varzine's pecan pie. He sat down with him while Shugg chased a squirrel. Carlton was respectful but reserved, a bit scared, to be honest, at the attention. He wondered why Charlie was talking to him, singling him out. Had he done something wrong? The lowest on the totem, was he going to be fired? Mac, the boss, wondered at it too.

Charlie soon learned that Carlton had quit school but got his high school diploma on line. He did this to be able to work in the day, to give his folks his paycheck to pay bills. The family had hit rock bottom and there were more bills. He'd wanted to go to college to study engineering and go to architecture school. Such were his wild dreams. Carlton told Charlie he figured that building with Mac was the closest he'd ever come to that dream. Carlton looked off into the distance and said, "That's life. It is what it is." Charlie smiled.

After a few weeks, Carlton and Charlie were easy with one another. Carlton had once taken supper with them. Nadeen remarked to Charlie that he cleaned up well in his Sunday suit.

She didn't recognize him at first. Miss Eustacia was at supper too. She had taught Carlton a class at school. She told Charlie he had been an exceptional student and she'd hated to hear he'd dropped out. All she knew was that there were financial problems at home. She was glad to learn he'd gotten his diploma on his own, but was not surprised that he could and would.

Little did the young man know, that after three months, when the building was finished and the men in their vans and trucks had evaporated and materialised at another job, he would remain. Charlie hired him to drive the family. Nadeen needed his help that way and the carrying in of heavy bags of groceries and supplies. They didn't use the word "chauffeur," but that's what he was. They just called him Carlton. He now lived in the little room over the garage. Charlie made a point of seeing him every day whether he needed him or not.

Hazel was in heaven. She had another fellow to dress, this time with casual sporty English tweedy clothes. She had his room furnished in antique architectural prints, a comfortable overstuffed chair for reading, and an oversized four-poster antique Charleston rice bed. Carlton needed that for his tall frame. He told Charlie that this was the first bed he'd ever had in which he could stretch out.

Charlie was trying him out, seeing if his instincts had served him correct, seeing for certain what stuff he was made of. He thought he already knew, but he'd learned from life that if you really wanted to know somebody well, you had to work with him or have him work for you.

Carlton didn't realize it yet, but his world was about to change in even more dramatic ways. Carlton passed all of Charlie's tests. He'd made his living there for a short time at the cars' steering wheels, but for him the momentous big wheel of Dame Fortune was about to turn.

A short year later, he would be enrolled at the College of Charleston and acing his courses—at the top of some of his classes, in fact—in preparation for admission to their architectural school.

He would take side courses in the city at the College of Building Arts to learn hands-on the lost traditional crafts of the trade. Working in stone and marble was his thing. Chiseling was hard and slow, but stone lasted. He thought *stonecutter* might be the highest name a craftsman could achieve. Something in him needed that kind of permanence. Charlie understood the feeling well. Both men gloried in patiently created detail and this provided another bond. Carlton, accustomed to manual labour as he had been for most of his young life, was already strong, but his forearms now were responding to his trade.

Charlie smiled and called him sybarite. "Fellow sybarite," he said, in the manner some would proffer a hand in a secret handshake or give a Masonic sign. Carlton didn't have to look up the word. He knew what it meant and took it for the compliment it was.

Charleston was full of good examples of classical architectural style. In this way it was an outdoor classroom for Carlton. Like his patron who made it possible to go to school without taking an evening job, his tastes inclined that way. He had time to devote to his studies and let the city help educate him. There was nothing like living in your subject. It was wrong to live in modern squalor and have to escape it by going to a museum or to look at the corpse of a thing in pictures or in an isolated lone example here and there with the barbaric shoddy in between.

For his graduation, Charlie, with Miss Eustacia's guidance, gave him John Ruskin's *The Stones of Venice* and Ruskin's volumes of architectural essays. It was Eustacia's Scots influence showing again. In fair exchange, Carlton introduced Charlie to Palladio, about whom he'd learned much in school. Like Jefferson centuries before, Charlie and Carlton found inspiration in his ordered designs and of what they said of man's possibilities. The Georgian period of symmetry and balance and harmony appealed to both of them. Thus began another new phase of collecting for the library.

For the celebration of the library building's completion, Charlie gave the growing collection a crowning glorious gift: Palladio's original Italian edition of his *Four Books of Architecture—Il Quattro Libre*. Not even Mr Jefferson had the original one. Miss Eustacia contributed her antebellum Legare Street family's leather bound early edition of Vetruvius.

There was a still greater surprise. It had taken some doing but through a London dealer in rare books, Charlie had acquired Shakespeare's second folio. The builders had followed Charlie's specifications and had fire-proofed the structure and given it U-V proof windows and state of the art climate control. Shakespeare had been his friend when friends were few. Now he'd take care of his friend. He took this duty personally. King Hal would have a safe home.

Of course, Miss Eustacia was pleased with all this. Each day was a joy. She was especially happy with Charlie and the man he'd become. One day she called him Larry de Medici. Charlie asked, "Larry who?" She wrote him a note addressed to the Doge of Venice. It began, "Dear Doge."

Charlie's crash course in western civilization still had its many gaps, in fact, some major black holes. But he looked things up and grasped what she meant. The word was "patronage." He had the central thrust right. Many of the peripheral niceties, however, were still missing to him. In conversation both inside and outside the house, he said proudly that he reckoned he could afford to help Carlton, that after all, he was one of the doggies of Venice. He imagined Shugg ensconced regally in the front seat of a flower-bedecked gondola, family banners flying.

Miss Eustacia couldn't help but laugh. The teacher corrected and explained. This being misunderstood in laughable ways was a professional hazard, the chance of which she was prepared to take, she said, but ever after, Charlie would never have it any other way. In word and deed, a doggie of Venice, he was, and remained.

Nineteen

Opening Doors

Charlie was very pleased with the way the library building had turned out. He'd now celebrated the second year anniversary of its opening with a quiet marking of the date. In honour of Miss Eustacia and her father he'd purchased the autographed Wessex Edition of Thomas Hardy's works.

After fourteen months of chauffeuring, Carlton had gone off to school, where he was digging in. In his sophomore year, he'd joined the South Carolina Historical Society, the Charleston Library Society and both preservation societies in town. Charlie had encouraged him to. He haunted the Historical Society on the ballast-stone Chalmers Street as much for the Greek revival building itself as for the wealth within. The reading room with its marble busts on alabaster pedestals felt like home. The stone images had become distant family. Whenever he felt at a loss and the city crowd of tourists and its noise were too much for him, he had this safe space, his cool and quiet retreat.

Once Charlie visited him there and immediately understood why Carlton felt this way. They talked about old and well-built structures such as this. Carlton surmised that buildings taught him as much as his professors, maybe more. He explained that a fine old building beyond representing memory and continuity told the truth. That's all it could do. A building had no vested interest, no job or salary to protect, no agenda to promote. It was silent testimony. Fine buildings were about more than power.

Carlton read Charlie a paragraph he'd found. Its gist was that if you had to trust the statistics of a culture or a building, you should trust the building. They both found that wise.

Charlie liked the way the architect of the building had respected its surroundings, how its scale and proportion were right. It stood in rhythm with its neighbours—the Gabriel Manigault-designed structure to its south and the Palladio-inspired colonial statehouse diagonally across Meeting. It was a good neighbour looking as if to say, I respect you and where I am and want to fit in. Charlie commented that modern structures too often wanted to scream attention to themselves, like a bratty adolescent, wanting to assert individuality and trying to be different sometimes as a shock and affront. They were reflections of their time. At this, Charlie, who had lately taken an interest in poet Ezra Pound, quoted him, "The Age Demanded an image of its accelerated grimace." Carlton understood.

At the middle of Carlton's second year at college, Nadeen and Charlie had their third child. This time, as the doctor had predicted, it was an easy birth. They'd refused to learn its sex by ultra-sound. Nadeen had said in her down to earth way, "What will be will be. I like surprises."

It was a third son. After careful thought, they named him Thomas-Lynn. They would call him Tommy-Lynn.

Nadeen attended St. Fiacre Church. She went with Hazel to early mass every Sunday, while Charlie and Varzine attended the babes. She'd then come home and go to eleven o'clock service with Charlie, while Hazel kept the babes. She felt it important that those who worked for them wouldn't be denied church. She'd dealt with that before coming to South Carolina. Once a month, she sang in the church choir. She had a fine soprano voice.

Miss Oma-Lynn had brought up Charlie in the First Baptist Church, but Nadeen was not comfortable in a service without a liturgy. Charlie took to the ancient liturgical forms immediately. They compromised in membership at All Saints Anglican. It was an old Southern pattern, often repeated as a natural progression. Born Methodist or Baptist, the successful ones eventually entered the Episcopal door. For Charlie and Nadeen, however, it was not a status thing, but a matter of liturgy, a simple matter, but not so simple after all if you took the liturgy seriously, as they both did. Hazel said in private that this was a good equation: Baptist plus Catholic equals Episcopal. In their case Anglican. They didn't like the modern iconoclastic and "progressive" Episcopal Church.

All Saints was one of those beautiful antebellum board and batten Gothic Revival structures relatively common in the Lowcountry. It sat shaded in its cool Spanish moss covered grove of patriarchal live oaks. Their limbs were home to a garden of resurrection fern. The church building had grown mellow with its century and a half of life. Its floors had been worn by the feet of the faithful despite earthquake, hurricane, invasion and war. It had seen its ups and downs, its ebb and flow of members. At one point around 1930, there were so few parishioners that they held church only once a month because they had to share a rector with two other far flung congregations.

This was Miss Eustacia's church. Her mother's people had gone to old St. Philip's Episcopal in Charleston. Her father's family was Presbyterian. In Kingstree, they'd chosen her mother's denomination. "Mama," she said, "was tired of gloom." The Presbyterian church there, was too Calvinistically inclined to suit her. Miss Eustacia said she received enough of that at home.

The growing flock of Gilyards sat in the same box pew with Miss Eustacia. It was there she had sat with her sister and their parents before. With her sister's death, their number had dwindled to one, but now counted seven, with Varzine and the Gilyards.

Nadeen thought the sacrament of infant baptism was important as her duty to the children. She felt Charlie's Baptist practice of adult baptism was a risky business. In their Anglican compromise, she was satisfied. Now that St Fiacre no longer used Latin, to her discomfort and chagrin, the churches weren't as different as she expected them to be. All Saints was a new break-away traditionalist congregation that had foresworn the recent watering downs of Episcopal doctrines and forms.

When they christened Tommy-Lynn, they baptized Charlie Jr., and Carlisle too. Carlton came home from college to be Tommy-Lynn's godfather. He was pleased despite their nixing the name he'd chosen for him. He finally agreed that no child in Kingstree should be saddled with Andrea Palladio as a given name.

Charlie feared to count his blessings. Reading Thomas Hardy had had its effect on him. Still, he sat looking at his family, blood and extended, now numbering nine: three lads, Nadeen and himself, Hazel, Varzine, and Carlton, and Miss Eustacia, who was like a mother to him and Nadeen. For the first time, he could look without dread into the future and could understand what the honoured titles *patriarch* and *pater familias* could mean. And yesterday, Nadeen had told him she might be expecting again. He had no doubt from his recent relishing more than usual a married man's ways, that there would soon be ten in the pew.

Some evenings he would come to All Saints and visit the church and cemetery in the quiet of dusk when no one was around. It had grown to be a favourite thing with him. The cemetery's moss-covered great oaks and magnolias had not been cut down as they had in so many cemeteries in this time of so-called progress. Their giant roots buckled two centuries of brick and slate paths, and twisted and grew into some of the iron palings on some of the fences of family plots. Here a giant white camellia had grown into a foot stone; there a large tea olive had coalesced with a marble slab. He liked the dark slate markers best of all. They were made by the stonecutter's art. These stones were for the village's founders who had slept there a century before the laying of the present building's corner stone. This was the third church on the site. The first was a colonial chapel-of-ease created by the South Carolina colony's Church Act of 1706.

The etched skulls and cherubs spoke to him in a mysterious language he didn't quite understand. He was inclining toward recognition, however, with each passing day. Sometimes Nadeen, he, and Carlton would come there together. Usually, few words, if any, were said.

Carlton was taking an extra course on his own now from the building arts school, where he'd made good progress in the old craft of carving slate. Charlie was the first to commission Carlton. Carlton had helped him design Charlie's headstone. Carlton had chosen the slab, shaped it, and had begun work on Charlie's name.

How quietly the dead lay there. In a way, they were Charlie's family too, although he was right in figuring that none of his blood kin was buried in its ground. Miss Eustacia's family was though. Her father, mother, sister, and brother lay in the row that extended the line of the church pew when they sat inside. The three centuries had filled almost every inch of the cemetery's soil. Charlie had just arranged with the rector the purchase of a small piece of available land that had just come up for sale adjacent to the cemetery's rear. In this new plot, he was the first to be assigned a burying place for his family. He wanted them together there.

The lessons of mutability and transience had not been lost on him. Today he came alone and stood on this newly purchased land. It was sodded in Charleston grass just beginning to take hold. He smiled at the truth that this was most definitely not portable property. He, or any one, could own many houses and thousands of acres of land, but the six-foot long plot was all they'd come to. It was the last door.

He didn't want to be embalmed. At least he'd bequeath worms an endowment to enrich the soil. He'd make certain the roots of a live oak newly planted by himself and Carlton would be his last beneficiary. It would encircle his bones and gather him in. Its limbs would shade him, Nadeen, and the ones they loved. With Nadeen's help, he'd already planted bulbs to naturalise.

Last week at dusk after the baptisms that morning, he and Nadeen had stood there at the tree and embraced. She totally got and approved what he was trying to do. At that moment, he loved and valued her more than at any time before. The years and the children were strengthening their bond.

He could only imagine the comfort Miss Eustacia felt with her family lying there. The colours of the splendid stained glass windows of All Saints when lit from within at night illuminated the vacant spot next to her sister that was ready to receive her. Charlie dreaded the day, but there was something very right about it all. In his mind, he drew the image of a circle rather than straight lines.

He could never feel the way Miss Eustacia felt about the cemetery, but she had taught him well John Keats's concept of negative capability, so he could enter into the feeling as if he were her, see life through her eyes, and feel it by proxy through her. He would will this ability direct to his children.

The heavy wrought iron gate creaked, then clanged behind him. A strand of grey moss touched his forehead and the neatly-trimmed bronze curls on his brow. Seen from a distance, it was like the setting sun burned them to the gold of a crown. Just as he had at his dining room table a few years before, he uttered quietly, *the meaning of peace*. He took a moment to give thanks, head bowed. *I am blessed*, he said aloud.

Tomorrow, he'd see about having Miss Oma-Lynn's remains moved from the memorial gardens on the four-lane outside town. It was one of those efficient, convenient perpetual care cemeteries that only allowed a small flat brass marker for each grave. Lawn mowers had to glide over the plots unimpeded by stones. She was lucky even to have that. That's all the money she had tucked away in her bureau drawer could buy. When he remembered how he found them at her request, the crumpled bills and coins saved with great sacrifice tugged at his heart. If she could only have lived to share his new life.

He suddenly felt her presence there in the quiet as dark descended on the sleepers. Maybe she did. Off in the distance in the village he could hear the clang and bells of trick-or-treaters going from door to door. How appropriate. It was All Saints Eve when the line between living and dead was erased.

In this new section of the cemetery, he'd have Miss Oma-Lynn reinterred and with a proper stone which he'd ask Carlton to carve. He would sleep by her in time.

Twenty

Celebration

It was a girl this time. They were all pleased. The three lads would now have a sister to love, tease, and protect. Charlie thought how he'd always wanted a sister himself and was happy for the boys. She was christened Olenska at All Saints on Whitsunday. It was Nadeen's mother's name. Nadeen sent dozens of pictures of their growing family to her folks. Things were still a bit dangerous back home, but much better these days. Soon they would be able to see one another again. They were already making plans.

The little girl's nickname quickly became Lennie to Junior, Lisle, and Tommy-Lynn. Hazel and Varzine were the next to adopt it, and then the rest of the family joined in.

Junior was now six and a half and a precocious little boy. He'd learned his abc's at three. To Charlie's dismay, he was already a computer whiz. They decided to limit his computer time to an hour a day. Miss Eustacia had started him on the usual first grade primers, just earlier, and now he was already up to Beatrix Potter, *Alice in Wonderland, Tom Brown's School Days, Uncle Remus,* and *Winnie the Pooh.* He was learning the Greek alphabet and rudimentary Greek words. Miss Eustacia remarked that it was wonderful to see how easily the very young could grasp a new language. She was reading him *Æsop's Tales* from her own well-worn copy that she had when she was learning Greek at about his age. She had just started him on Latin.

The couple had decided to school the children at home. When Charlie designed the library building, he'd had this in mind. A small side room held desks, a black board, the inevitable computer hookups, and a screen.

Miss Eustacia had agreed to tutor the boys. She had sold her house and was now living permanently with them. That just made sense. She was spending all her time there anyway. Charlie was so pleased that they'd have the good counsel of one that meant so much to him. With his, Carlton's, and Nadeen's help, the four were doing an excellent job of schooling the children. Nadeen noticed that Miss Eustacia looked like she'd grown many years younger and it was more than hair style and the flower-print dress. Nadeen commented to Hazel that Eustacia's new dresses made her look like spring after a hard grey winter. Carlton overheard and mumbled *Primavera*, the meaning of which was incomprehensible to those gathered. They didn't ask for an explanation, for Carlton did that sort of thing a lot and they just left the inexplicable alone with the thought, "That's just Carlton." They knew his ways.

Carlton was back home now with his degree. He was living over the garage again in his old quarters which he designed and reworked into an ensuite. He had a decent architectural business in Charleston which Charlie had helped him set up. He spent three days there a week and was about to hire an assistant newly graduated from the College of Building Arts. His restored office on East Bay had a bedroom, bath, and kitchen fitted into the third floor so he could stay in town and not use precious fossil fuel and even more precious time in a commute.

He'd already begun to impress the large and influential preservation set in town with several jobs on upper King. His specialty was restoration and Charleston and vicinity was an ideal place for that. His expertise filled a growing need as Charleston's preservation focus spread up the historic Neck that connected the peninsular city to the mainland. He was encouraged by the established restoration firms who welcomed another promising new talent on the scene. There was ample work to go around and Carlton was an affable, honest, clean cut young man. Hazel was dressing him too and he turned some heads at the functions he attended. At the parties in the heat of summer at the old houses in town, he wore short pants with his blazer and tie, as was the local custom for some of the young. He was a young man of his time and had to have a tattoo. It was a Greek key band that encircled his calf above the sock line. He was already considered one of the most eligible bachelors in town.

Charlie had hired him on Mondays and Fridays to preside over the library. He had set up a drafting table there for working on his designs. Nadeen declared that the hand-coloured sheets were fine works of art. Miss Eustacia agreed. He had always been a steady and patient fellow from the days Charlie had watched him on the construction crew. He took great pains with details. The natural light in the library was perfect for him. He had an excellent eye refined by his college minor in art history. His great love was Italian Renaissance Art. Botticelli was his favourite. There in the library he also tutored the lads for several hours twice a week. For recreation, he carved stone.

Miss Eustacia said she'd rarely seen anyone take to teaching so readily as he. In that, his remarkable patience was also the key. He taught the boys their math and elementary sciences, including one of his and Charlie's new interests—botany. Carlton had just begun sketching plans for a garden around Varzine and Eustacia's house and between his rooms and the library. He was glad the property had ten acres, enough for a large kitchen and good-size veggie patch, Nadeen's dream. She and Charlie had just finished reading *Candide*. From its pages, "Cultivate your own garden," had become a recent pet phrase. Charlie, however, didn't care very much for the rest of Voltaire. In fact, he soundly disapproved.

Miss Eustacia taught reading, writing, Latin, and French. Charlie and Carlton were learning Latin along with the lads. It was comic to see the two strapping grown men try to fit in side-arm desks.

Nadeen taught the boys art, such art as it was. She and Miss Eustacia agreed you couldn't start them too young. The same was particularly true of languages too. It was interesting to see how Junior learned his Latin much more quickly than his dad. Miss Eustacia thought Carlisle might have some talent in art. Time would tell. Charlie Jr. definitely did not. His talent inclined to building things, in which Carlton encouraged and helped him along.

Charlie taught them history, but mainly read stories to them. He had a gentle, good voice and read with conviction as if he'd written every word. Those sessions were the boys' favourite part of school. Nadeen had her private notion that it was because it was done by their dad. She'd never seen children so devoted as they were to him.

The number of books on the library shelves continued to grow. Miss Eustacia had now contributed all but a few of her books to its shelves. With such a library, there was no need for either public or private school. Next year, they'd bring in a tutor in music once a week. Carlton was already excited about introducing the boys to art history. They'd see where the children's main interests and talents lay and would nurture wherever and whenever they could.

The children had playmates of their own age from Sunday and Bible School. Nadeen saw to it that they were involved in church life. That was a particularly good thing for them because they were being home schooled.

When Charlie looked at his life, sometimes he had to hold his breath. Surely his life was charmed, and the spell would soon break. Against that breaking, he did everything a man could. He knew from experience that all played a deadly serious game with odds stacked against a man. He consciously strove to improve his odds. Any smart person would.

Nadeen had to remind him. Today he would be thirty-two. They would celebrate. The word sounded strange to his ears. In came the cake with thirty-two candles, one of Varzine's six-layer fresh grated coconut caramel masterpieces. Charlie said a cake wasn't good unless it weighed twenty pounds and dripped. This one may have tipped the scale at twenty-five. Charlie declared it a masterpiece. He had never had a birthday cake before.

Hazel said it was about time.

They all sat together at the big dining table. It was one of Carlton's days to be in Charleston, but he had stayed home. Charlie had wondered, but now he knew why. The number at table was ten. He looked at the six vacant chairs and recounted to himself his plans for filling some of them.

One would not be his father, however. The detective had given up the search a year ago. There was an ache in Charlie's heart, but he'd learned to heal it with other things. He hated he'd failed, but perhaps it was just as well. In this, and this only, he'd go it alone. It could be done. It had to be done. He would be to his children what his father had not been to him. He would be to Nadeen what his father had not been to his mother.

Not a bad percentage of successes though, he said to himself as the words to 'Happy Birthday' were pathetically sung, in a way to cause Shugg who was under the table to howl, or maybe just join in. The lads tried to sing but forgot half the words. Carlton flatted loudly along. He could never be accused of carrying a tune. Charlie laughed at the cacophony and looked at his friend with his little party hat on…the brother he'd never had. He felt that no man could ask for a better friend.

Nadeen's birthday gift to Charlie was her announcement that the doctor just last week had declared her pregnant with their fifth child. Charlie's face flushed red with joy. He didn't say anything but rose and guided her to his seat at the head of the table. The timing was perfect and made his declaration of his own gift to the household all the more appropriate.

He'd quietly lined up six likely prospects for Hazel and Varzine to interview. Each woman would pick one. This way there'd be no chance for a dispute over which to choose. The two would come in and help each woman five days a week. With his growing household, he knew this would take a real load off Nadeen and them. The two new women would live at their own homes in town.

There was a hard-case lady raising her children as a single parent. Charlie had already decided that if Hazel and Varzine didn't choose her, he'd hire her himself and figure out later what she could do. She loved to garden, so she might be in charge of the gardens now growing under Carlton and his part-time gardener's hands.

No indeed, in the heart of this fond gathering, Charlie was no longer alone. He reckoned what his life's trajectory had been. It was clearly a journey to joining in.

This was Miss Eustacia's first celebration in many a decade. Charlie was real pleased with her gift to him of a 1750 edition of *Tom Jones* in the original hand-tooled leather volumes. It had been passed down in her family and belonged to her kin. Charlie had read the novel in a big falling apart paperback a second time. He still identified with the main character and life's miraculous reversal of things, but had grown to like Squire Western best of all. Now he looked forward to a third reading, this time in the neat little four volume set just as it had looked to the eyes of its readers over two and a half centuries ago. The book had first been owned by Robert Marion, the famous Swamp Fox's elder brother. The first volume bore Robert's signature dated from Santee Parish, S C, and that of Peter Porcher Jnr. on the title page. The work had personal meaning to both Miss Eustacia and him because it was the second long work she'd suggested he read.

Birthday parties were a new thing in Charlie's life. He thought them a good thing. Nadeen and the children from now on would have their own. Five children! It made his head spin.

Like Charlie, Carlton had had few celebrations in his short years, but his life was now opening outward. He'd met a woman his age from the farm country south of town. While in high school before he was old enough to work in construction, he had sometimes made precious money for his family as a groom's assistant at a stable there. He loved horses, and though he'd not been given much opportunity to ride, he still enjoyed being around horses and the company of people who gathered around.

Mary Beth Sinkler was a talented rider. She was the daughter of the stable owner who had employed him. Carlton had met her there when he was sixteen. In college, she'd been on the equestrian team. He was courting her now. She was a member of the Cedar Swamp Lancers, a club that held an improbable impressive medieval joust each fall and spring. She was teaching Carlton to ride. She noted that it didn't take him very long to sit up impressively straight in the saddle. At his desk so often, he needed this contrast in his life.

So did Charles. Carlton and Mary Beth had introduced him around, and the two were looking to purchase and stable thoroughbreds at Carlton's old grooming ground. Charles didn't relish riding, in fact refused to, but Carlton's friends were jolly and cordial and he liked the joust. It reminded him of the Chevalier Bayard. He learned from them and Miss Eustacia how big the tournaments had been in the Lowcountry before the war. They had taken their lead from Sir Walter Scott's *Ivanhoe*.

The Lancers had good bar-b-que's. There was something so right about eating outdoors with them—a joy Charlie had not experienced or even imagined before. They'd have pig-pickings with Frogmore stew. The famous pit-master came from a nearby community. He'd been slow-cooking local Ossabaw pig over hickory coals since he was twelve years old. When asked, he gave the corny answer that his main ingredient was love. But that was at least half true. Through the joust and the eating together, Charlie realized how close all these friends became.

It was the communal celebration of the bond forged by sharing food that was as old as civilised man. Carlton and Charlie were learning the meaning of belonging, a key something that had been lacking in their lives and they didn't even know. The knowledge gained so far had already made them better men. God willing, they would pass it on to their children. In Carlton's case, Mary Beth was keen on that. She said children and horses would be her career.

So Charlie reckoned that this birthday party was in some ways not after all a completely new thing. It was a true celebration like those the Lancers had invited him to, and this past year Charlie had already made up his mind to relish life like they did and in the right ways. You couldn't do it properly alone, a thing he reckoned he'd not ever be again.

The only shadow over Charlie's mind as he looked at his little ones and his growing family was the sudden brief fleeting image of Hardy's pitiful little character, Jude's ill-fated son, who hanged himself with the note "Because we are too many," that is, too many for his family to feed. He pondered the conclusion he'd come to, the one Hardy's novel had not. A child was given the greatest gift of all, of life itself, no matter how tragically short the life and its outcome. Still, "Jude's little boy," "Jude's little boy," he found himself repeating to himself amid the hoopla of birthday whistles and bells. He'd been near that desperation himself in the dark times, that now seemed so far away.

Sensing perhaps something of her master's mood, Shugg came out from under the table and sat by his side looking at him. She rested her head against his knee. Charlie stroked her head, and asked for another slice of cake. Nadeen had risen and stood behind Charlie and gave the top of his curls the brush of a kiss. He squeezed her hand.

"A side piece this time, with lots of icing," he said. After a pause, he added, "Making up for lost time," as he looked first at Nadeen and then at Varzine, who couldn't have been more pleased.

Epilogue

To Mister Rodger MacManus
From Mister Loutrell Decimus Heywood

Sonnyboy,

How long you goin to stay way down there in Arkansas? All your folks is about to write your obituary and divide up your clothes and fishing lures.

We have had <u>some</u> doings lately. Old mister Chance Stately has been on a rampage. Seems he done got in the Hairloom Seed Saving business and got to planting an old watermelon that is as white as the driven snow. Gets over 60 pound. It's nice and smooth and shaped like a humongous egg.

Mister Chance has the purtiest field this side of Barnwell. You ought to see them melons bobbing up from on top the vines like corks on a pond of pickerel weed.

They are Mister Chance's pride and joy—that is, they <u>was</u>, till a fellow all the way from Knoxville Tennessee showed up here unannounced and mysterious. We finely got his name out of him— Gene Harrowgate, kin to them McCarthys up there.

Well, this here Gene somehow heard of them snow-white watermelons all the way up in Tennessee. I've now got to know him well and he's telling me a lot about things, personal and otherwise. He says he was tired of green melons and that a white melon made him feel more normal like. "Good luck on that, ole hoss," I said.

That Gene is a caution. He knew when to strike and when not to. So Mister Chance enlisted the help of the game warden to do patrol. Like I told Chance, I wouldn't trust that game warden as far as I could throw him, and he's a big overweight fellow at that. He had good reason not to, let me tell you. Chance then had Deputy Doolittle patrol the patroller that was patrolling the field.

And guess who was watching all this from a deer stand in a sweetgum tree. None but Gene Harrowgate. On one full moon night last week, Gene woke up startled from his usual doze in the tree stand and saw a big melon move in the vines. He said it like to make him fall out of the tree, a thing he done oncet before and didn't want to do no time again. He wiped his eyes with his fist, and no mistaking, it moved again. Gene says it wasn't nothing but Deputy Doolittle's fat rear goin to town.

Gene says the sight has cured him complete. He has nightmares about it still. Tells me he's out of the watermelon business for certain sure. He climbed down out of that stand, walked out of that field, and didn't stop til he got to Elloree. He says, Lord-a-mercy, that's a sight I never wants to see agin.

If the whole world gets in on the action, it aint no fun anymore, he declared. Says he's gonna go talk to our ole friend Charlie T.—that is, Mr. Charles Thomas Gilyard, Sr., excuse me, and see how he might learn to settle down and get on a better road to a place he could stay put in. Always striking out for the territories gets a mite old. Told him, you got a great idea ole hoss, if civilising is what you wants and needs to be. There aint no better man to call on than Mr. Charles Thomas Gilyard, Sr. He's shore been thar before.

Best get on in to supper. Smell them hot cat-head biscuits and collard greens. Whoo-ee!

Yore ever devoted friend,

Mr. Loutrell Decimus Heywood

About the Author

JAMES KIBLER was born in Prosperity, South Carolina and graduated from the University of South Carolina with a Ph.D. in English. His interests have lead him to write on diverse subjects, from botany and agriculture to architecture and art. As literary man, he has written in several genres, including the novel, short story, and poetry. The history and saga of the renovation of his plantation house is chronicled in his critically acclaimed *Our Fathers' Fields*, which was awarded the prestigious Fellowship of Southern Writers Award for Nonfiction.

It is rare for a writer to excel as both a creative artist and a scholar, but Kibler has achieved such distinction. For many years Professor of English at the University of Georgia, he has written authoritatively on many aspects of Southern literature. As scholar, Kibler is largely responsible for the contemporary rise of William Gilmore Simms studies. He is the founding editor of *Simms Review*, author of the definitive work on Simms's poetry, and the discoverer of many previously unknown Simms writings.

The Gentler Gamester is Kibler's fifth novel. He has just completed his second volume of poetry, *In the Deep Heart's Core: Poems of Tribute and Remembrance*, due from Shotwell Publishing later this year.

Available From Green Altar Books

If you enjoyed this book, perhaps some of our other titles will pique your interest. The following titles are now available for your reading pleasure... Enjoy!

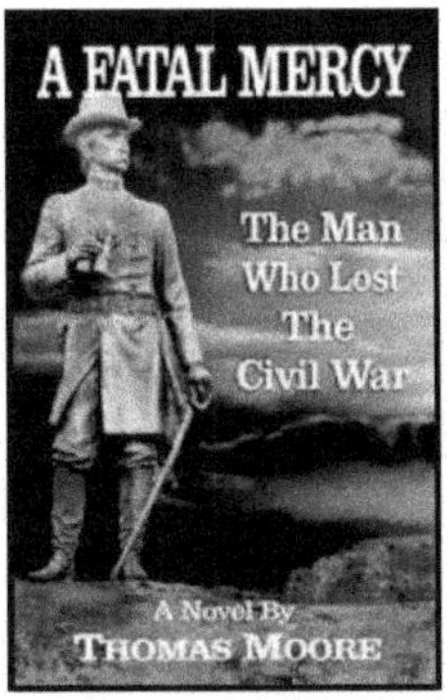

Green Altar (Literary Imprint)

Catharine Brosman
An Aesthetic Education and Other Stories (2nd Ed)

Chained Tree, Chained Owls: Poems

Aerosols and Other Poems

Randall Ivey
A New England Romance: And Other Southern Stories

Suzanne Johnson
Maxcy Gregg's Sporting Journals 1842-1858

James E. Kibler, Jr.
Tiller : Claybank County Series, Vol. 4

The Gentler Gamester

In the Deep Heart's Core: Poems of Tribute and Remembrance (forthcoming)

Thomas Moore
A Fatal Mercy: The Man Who Lost The Civil War

Perrin Lovett
The Substitute, Tom Ironsides 1

Karen Stokes
Belles

Carolina Twilight

Honor in the Dust

The Immortals

The Soldier's Ghost: A Tale of Charleston

William Thomas
Runaway Haley: An Imagined Family Saga

The Field of Justice: Moonshine and Murder in North Georgia

Gold-Bug
(Mystery & Suspense Imprint)

Brandi Perry
Splintered: A New Orleans Tale

Martin Wilson
To Jekyll and Hide

www.ingramcontent.com/pod-product-compliance
Ingram Content Group UK Ltd.
Pitfield, Milton Keynes, MK11 3LW, UK
UKHW021326180426
11947UKWH00017B/1461